Roba

Billy & Buddy

IT'S A DOG'S LIFE

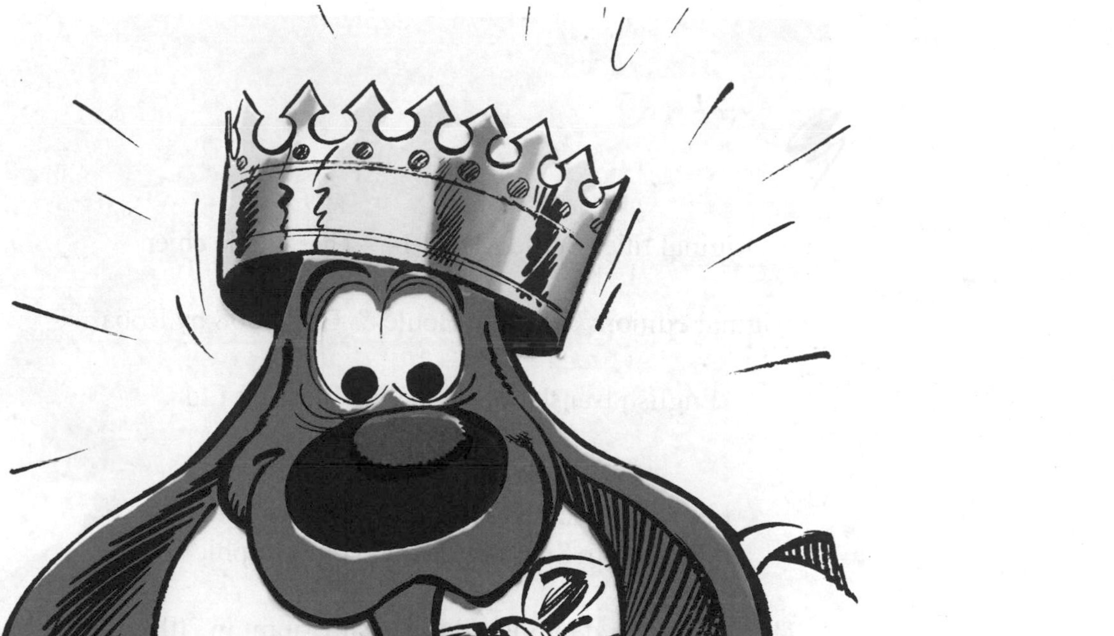

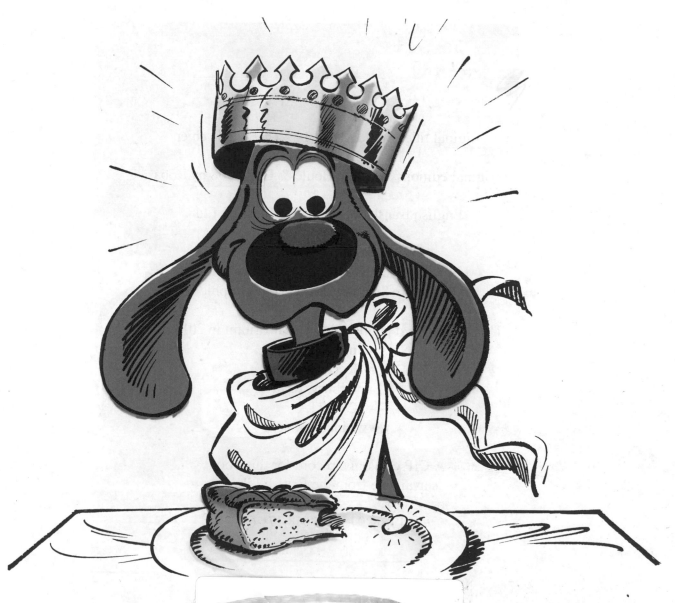

Original title: Boule & Bill 14 – Une vie de chien

Original edition: © Studio Boule & Bill, 2008 by Roba

English translation: © 2013 Cinebook Ltd

Translator: Jerome Saincantin
Lettering and text layout: Design Amorandi
Printed in Spain by Just Colour Graphic

This edition first published in Great Britain in 2013 by
Cinebook Ltd
56 Beech Avenue
Canterbury, Kent
CT4 7TA
www.cinebook.com

A CIP catalogue record for this book
is available from the British Library

ISBN 978-1-84918-171-6

9th CINEBOOK
The 9th Art Publisher

Milking it for all it's worth

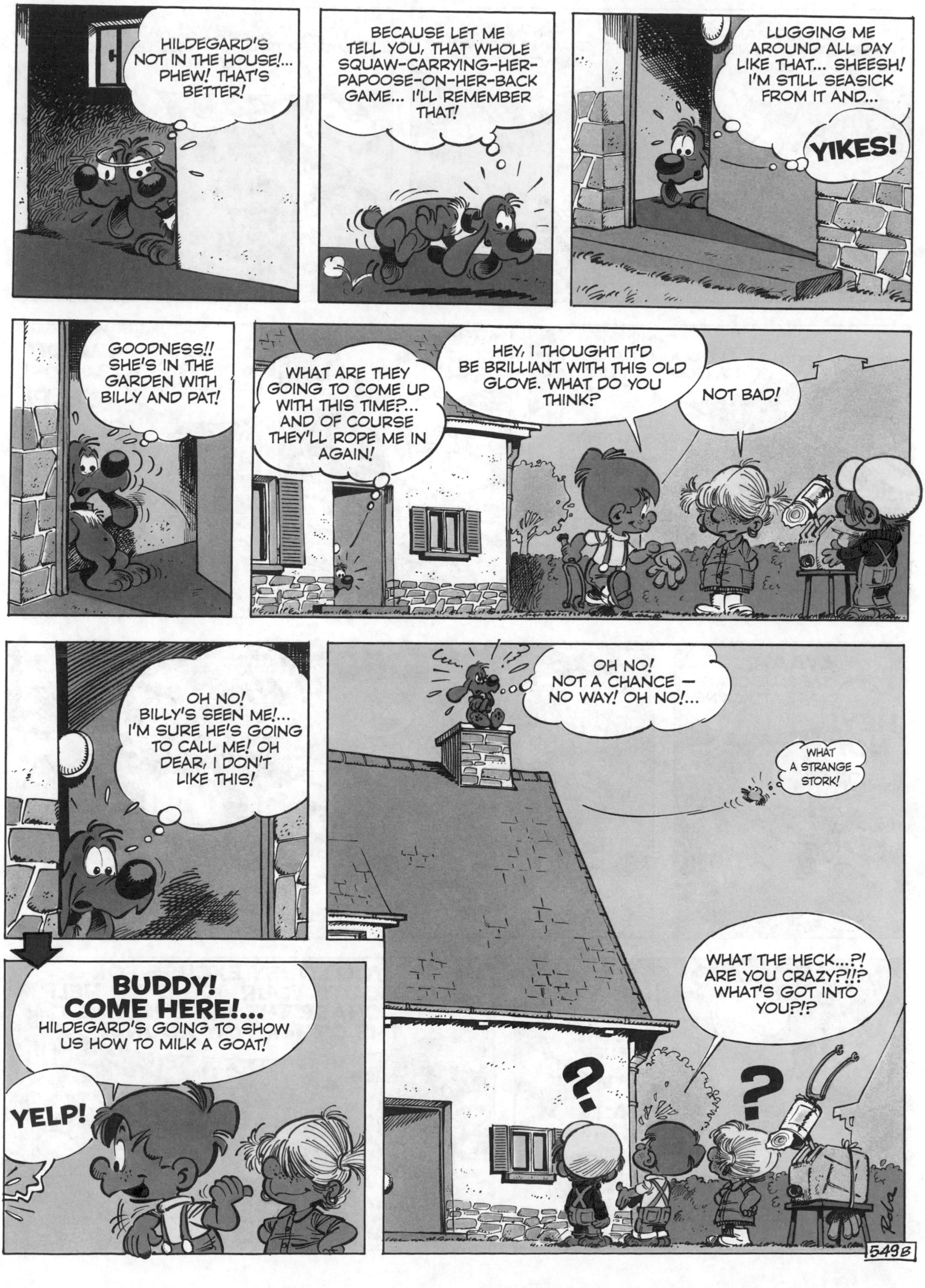
HILDEGARD'S NOT IN THE HOUSE!... PHEW! THAT'S BETTER!
BECAUSE LET ME TELL YOU, THAT WHOLE SQUAW-CARRYING-HER-PAPOOSE-ON-HER-BACK GAME... I'LL REMEMBER THAT!
LUGGING ME AROUND ALL DAY LIKE THAT... SHEESH! I'M STILL SEASICK FROM IT AND...
YIKES!
GOODNESS!! SHE'S IN THE GARDEN WITH BILLY AND PAT!
WHAT ARE THEY GOING TO COME UP WITH THIS TIME?... AND OF COURSE THEY'LL ROPE ME IN AGAIN!
HEY, I THOUGHT IT'D BE BRILLIANT WITH THIS OLD GLOVE. WHAT DO YOU THINK?
NOT BAD!
OH NO! BILLY'S SEEN ME!... I'M SURE HE'S GOING TO CALL ME! OH DEAR, I DON'T LIKE THIS!
BUDDY! COME HERE!... HILDEGARD'S GOING TO SHOW US HOW TO MILK A GOAT!
YELP!
OH NO! NOT A CHANCE — NO WAY! OH NO!...
WHAT A STRANGE STORK!
WHAT THE HECK...?! ARE YOU CRAZY?!!? WHAT'S GOT INTO YOU?!?
?
?
549B

Cavalry

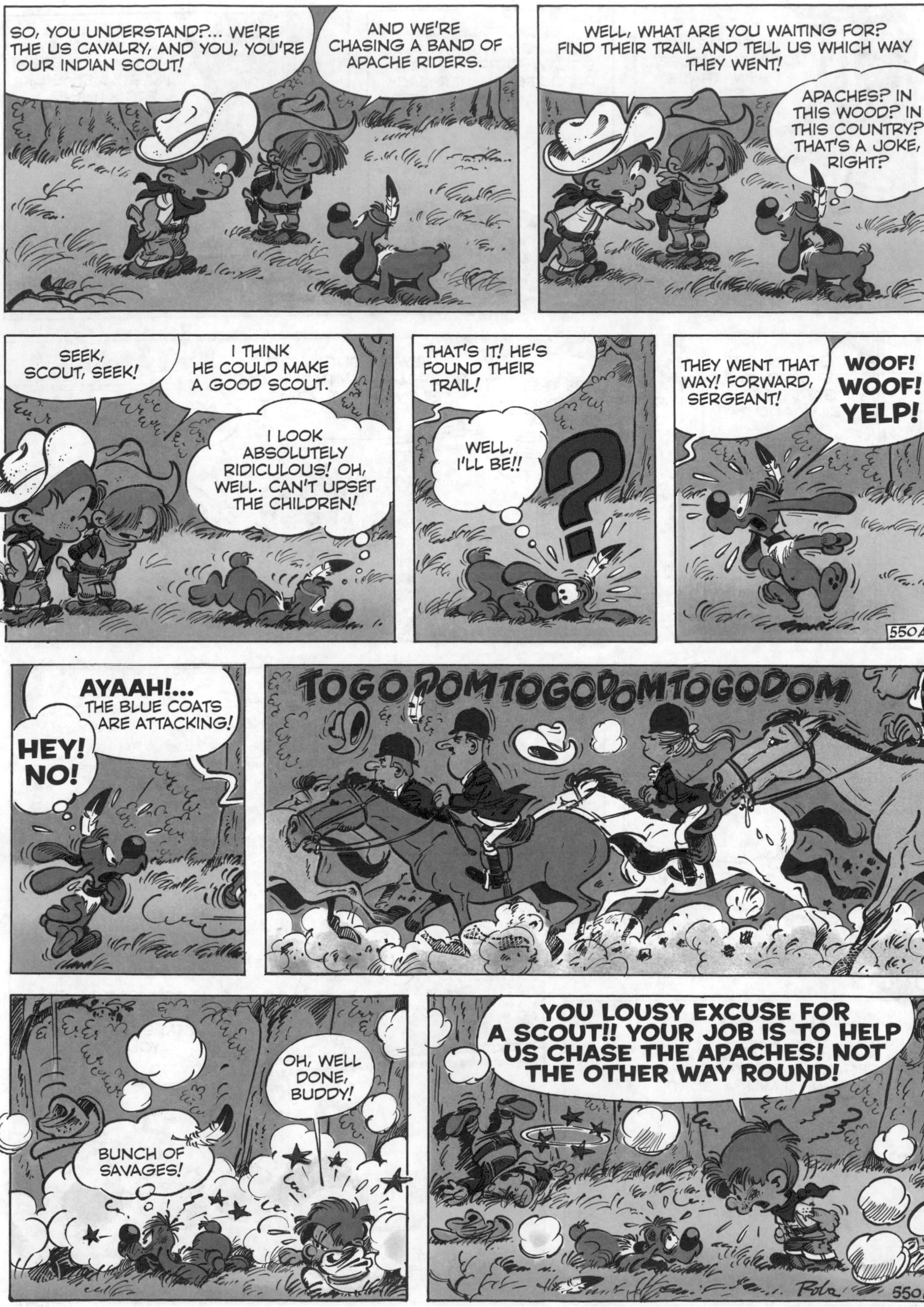

SO, YOU UNDERSTAND?... WE'RE THE US CAVALRY, AND YOU, YOU'RE OUR INDIAN SCOUT!
AND WE'RE CHASING A BAND OF APACHE RIDERS.
WELL, WHAT ARE YOU WAITING FOR? FIND THEIR TRAIL AND TELL US WHICH WAY THEY WENT!
APACHES? IN THIS WOOD? IN THIS COUNTRY? THAT'S A JOKE, RIGHT?
SEEK, SCOUT, SEEK!
I THINK HE COULD MAKE A GOOD SCOUT.
I LOOK ABSOLUTELY RIDICULOUS! OH, WELL. CAN'T UPSET THE CHILDREN!
THAT'S IT! HE'S FOUND THEIR TRAIL!
WELL, I'LL BE!!
?
THEY WENT THAT WAY! FORWARD, SERGEANT!
WOOF! WOOF! YELP!
550A
AYAAH!... THE BLUE COATS ARE ATTACKING!
HEY! NO!
TOGODOMTOGODOMTOGODOM
OH, WELL DONE, BUDDY!
BUNCH OF SAVAGES!
YOU LOUSY EXCUSE FOR A SCOUT!! YOUR JOB IS TO HELP US CHASE THE APACHES! NOT THE OTHER WAY ROUND!
Roba
550B

Poisonous business

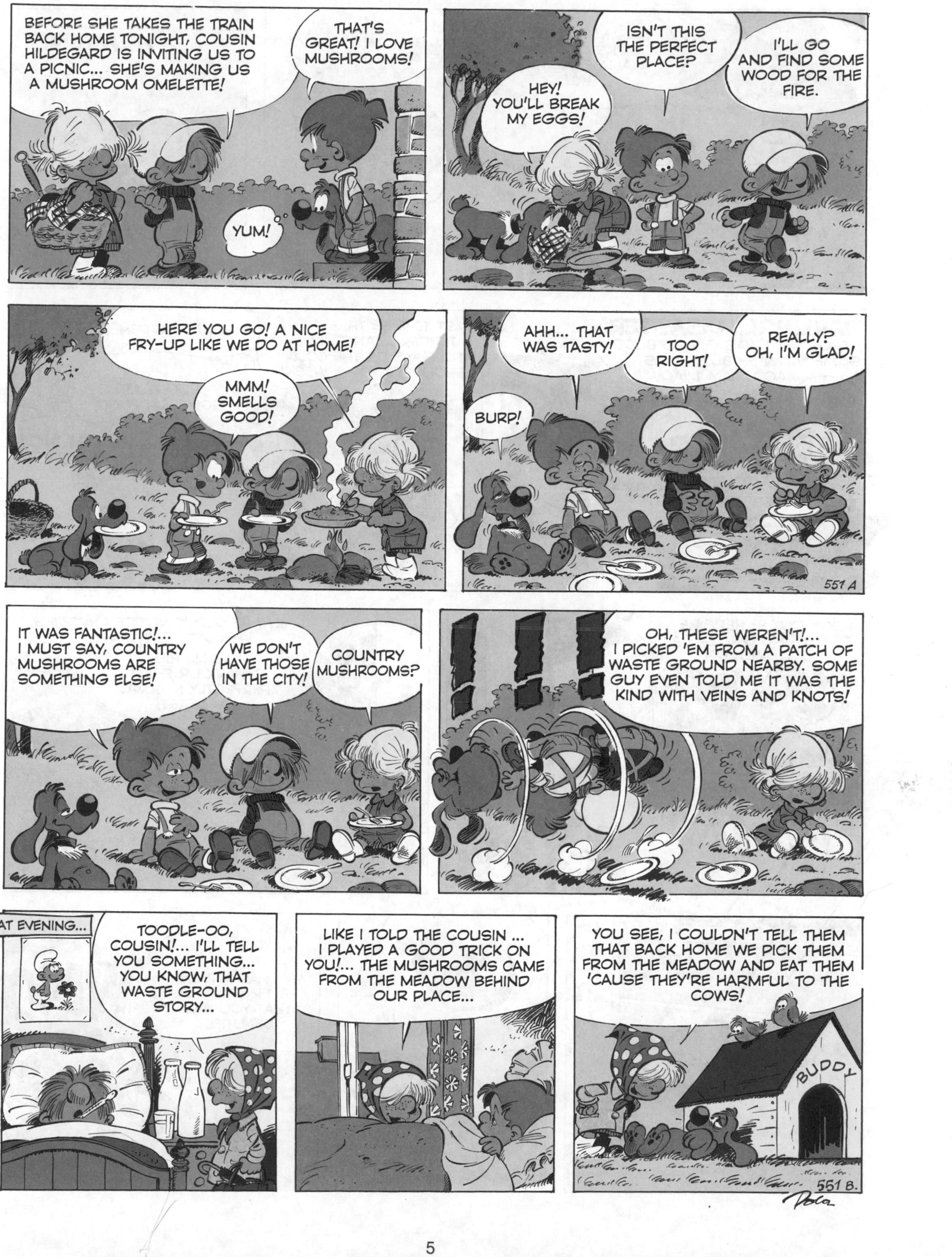
BEFORE SHE TAKES THE TRAIN BACK HOME TONIGHT, COUSIN HILDEGARD IS INVITING US TO A PICNIC... SHE'S MAKING US A MUSHROOM OMELETTE!
THAT'S GREAT! I LOVE MUSHROOMS!
YUM!
ISN'T THIS THE PERFECT PLACE?
HEY! YOU'LL BREAK MY EGGS!
I'LL GO AND FIND SOME WOOD FOR THE FIRE.
HERE YOU GO! A NICE FRY-UP LIKE WE DO AT HOME!
MMM! SMELLS GOOD!
AHH... THAT WAS TASTY!
TOO RIGHT!
REALLY? OH, I'M GLAD!
BURP!
551 A
IT WAS FANTASTIC!... I MUST SAY, COUNTRY MUSHROOMS ARE SOMETHING ELSE!
WE DON'T HAVE THOSE IN THE CITY!
COUNTRY MUSHROOMS?
OH, THESE WEREN'T!... I PICKED 'EM FROM A PATCH OF WASTE GROUND NEARBY. SOME GUY EVEN TOLD ME IT WAS THE KIND WITH VEINS AND KNOTS!
THAT EVENING...
TOODLE-OO, COUSIN!... I'LL TELL YOU SOMETHING... YOU KNOW, THAT WASTE GROUND STORY...
LIKE I TOLD THE COUSIN ... I PLAYED A GOOD TRICK ON YOU!... THE MUSHROOMS CAME FROM THE MEADOW BEHIND OUR PLACE...
YOU SEE, I COULDN'T TELL THEM THAT BACK HOME WE PICK THEM FROM THE MEADOW AND EAT THEM 'CAUSE THEY'RE HARMFUL TO THE COWS!
BUDDY
551 B.
Roba

Mutation

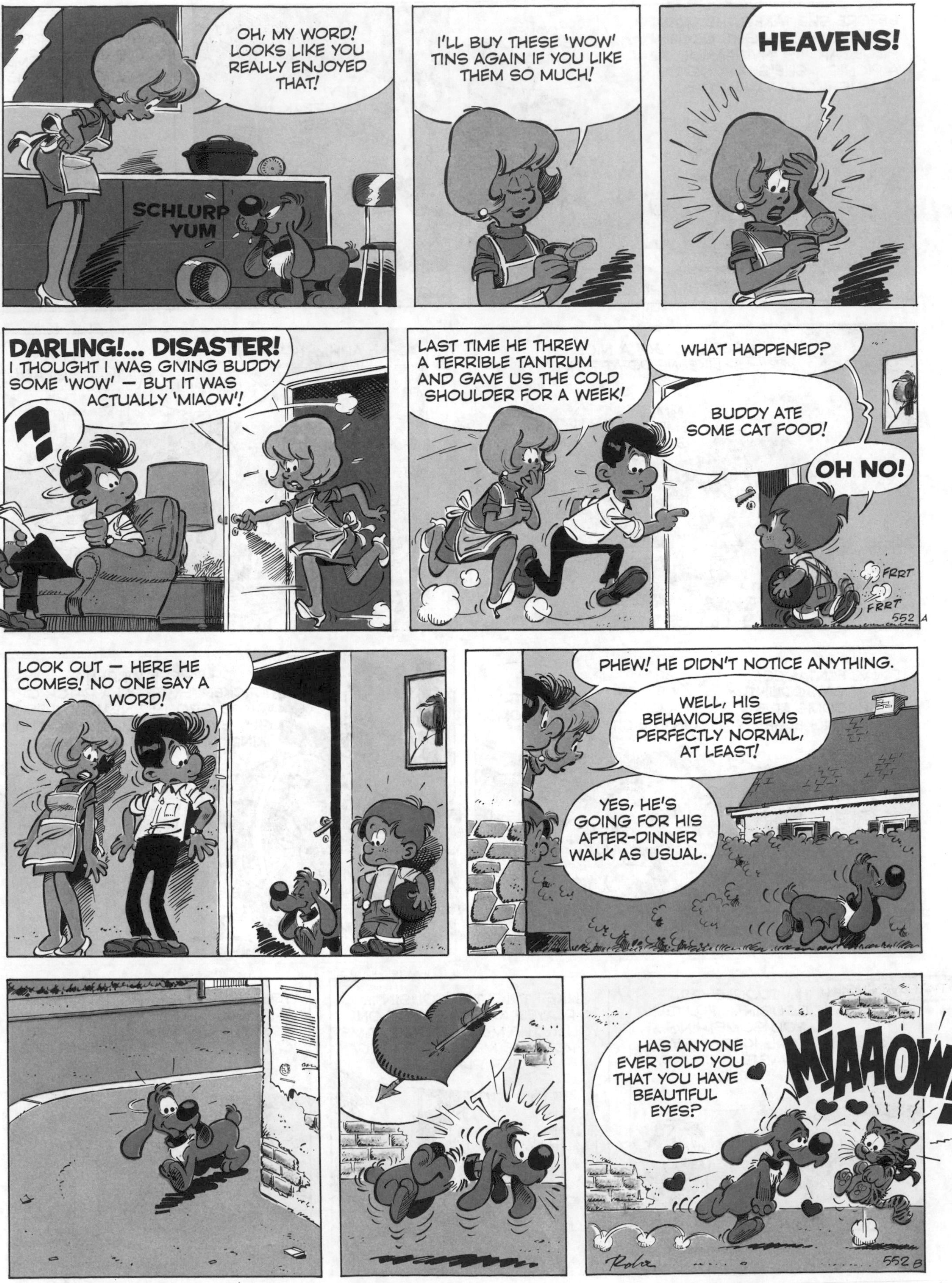
OH, MY WORD! LOOKS LIKE YOU REALLY ENJOYED THAT!
SCHLURP
YUM
I'LL BUY THESE 'WOW' TINS AGAIN IF YOU LIKE THEM SO MUCH!
HEAVENS!
DARLING!... DISASTER! I THOUGHT I WAS GIVING BUDDY SOME 'WOW' — BUT IT WAS ACTUALLY 'MIAOW'!
?
LAST TIME HE THREW A TERRIBLE TANTRUM AND GAVE US THE COLD SHOULDER FOR A WEEK!
WHAT HAPPENED?
BUDDY ATE SOME CAT FOOD!
OH NO!
FRRT
FRRT
552 A
LOOK OUT — HERE HE COMES! NO ONE SAY A WORD!
PHEW! HE DIDN'T NOTICE ANYTHING.
WELL, HIS BEHAVIOUR SEEMS PERFECTLY NORMAL, AT LEAST!
YES, HE'S GOING FOR HIS AFTER-DINNER WALK AS USUAL.
HAS ANYONE EVER TOLD YOU THAT YOU HAVE BEAUTIFUL EYES?
MIAAOW!
Roba
552 B

Lights, camera, action!

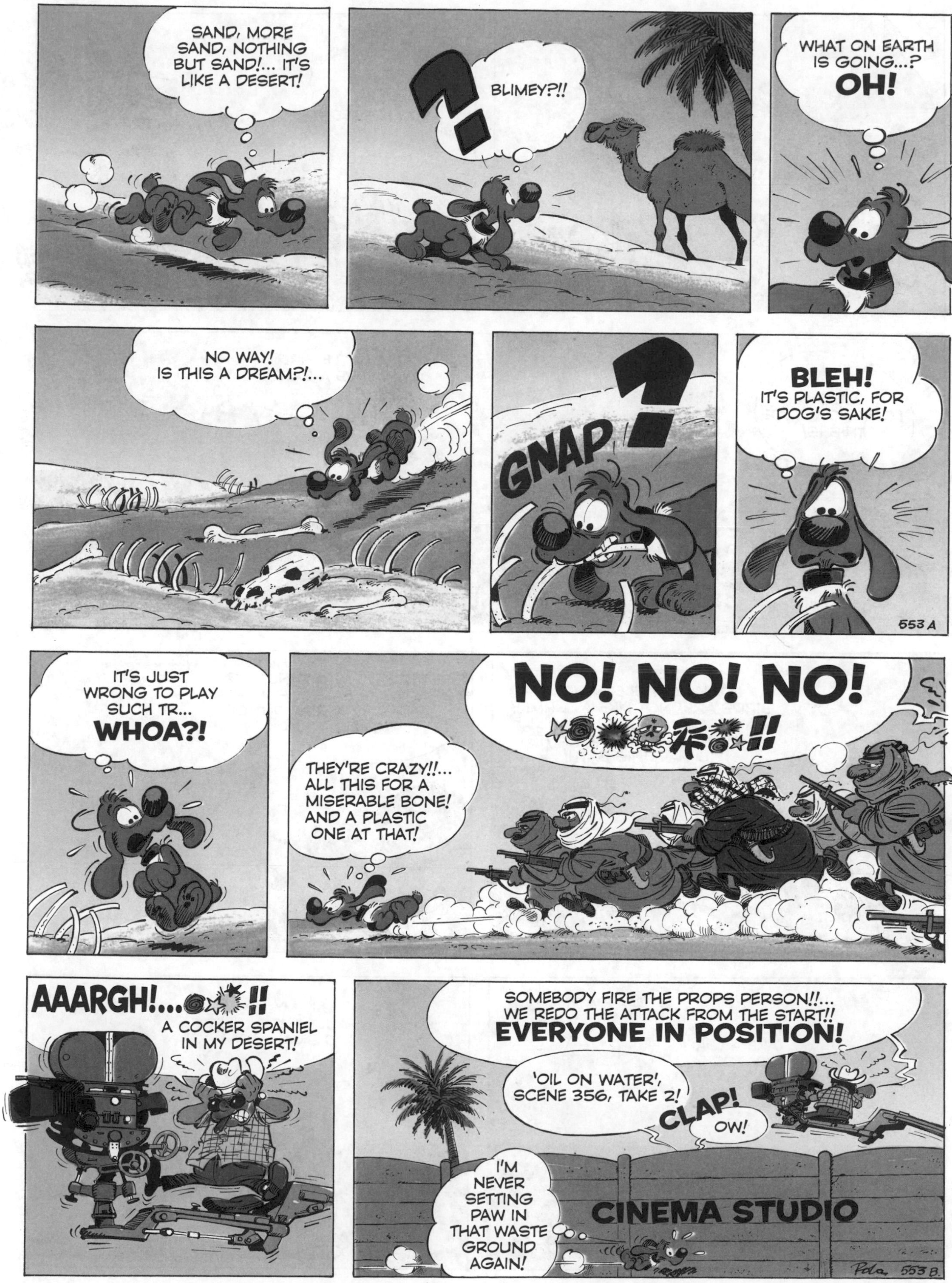

SAND, MORE SAND, NOTHING BUT SAND!... IT'S LIKE A DESERT!
BLIMEY?!!
WHAT ON EARTH IS GOING...? OH!
NO WAY! IS THIS A DREAM?!...
GNAP
BLEH! IT'S PLASTIC, FOR DOG'S SAKE!
553 A
IT'S JUST WRONG TO PLAY SUCH TR... WHOA?!
NO! NO! NO!
THEY'RE CRAZY!!... ALL THIS FOR A MISERABLE BONE! AND A PLASTIC ONE AT THAT!
AAARGH!... !!
A COCKER SPANIEL IN MY DESERT!
SOMEBODY FIRE THE PROPS PERSON!!... WE REDO THE ATTACK FROM THE START!! EVERYONE IN POSITION!
'OIL ON WATER', SCENE 356, TAKE 2!
CLAP!
OW!
I'M NEVER SETTING PAW IN THAT WASTE GROUND AGAIN!
CINEMA STUDIO
Roba 553 B.

Bath problems

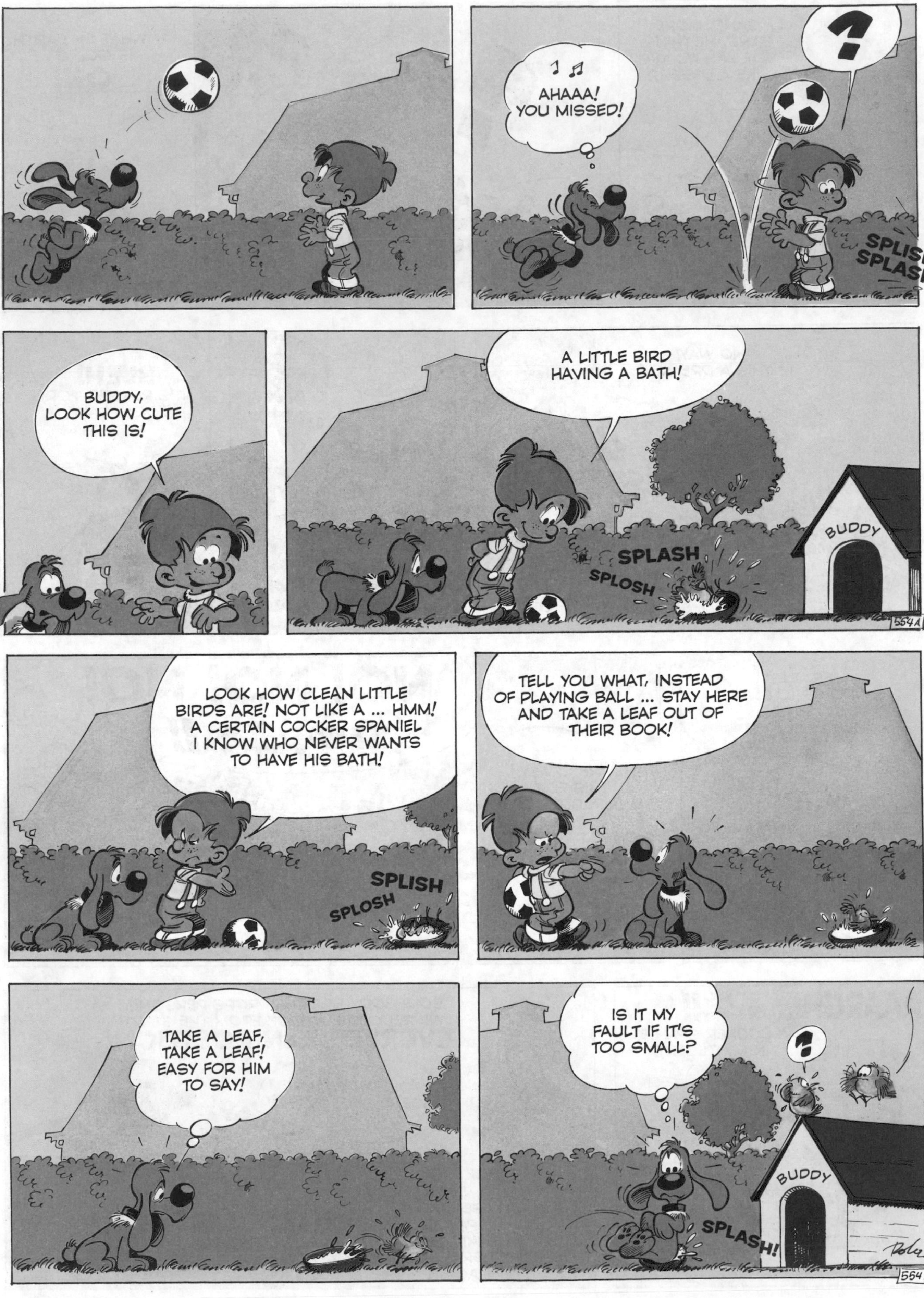
AHAAA! YOU MISSED!
?
SPLISH SPLASH
BUDDY, LOOK HOW CUTE THIS IS!
A LITTLE BIRD HAVING A BATH!
SPLASH
SPLOSH
BUDDY
554A
LOOK HOW CLEAN LITTLE BIRDS ARE! NOT LIKE A ... HMM! A CERTAIN COCKER SPANIEL I KNOW WHO NEVER WANTS TO HAVE HIS BATH!
SPLISH
SPLOSH
TELL YOU WHAT, INSTEAD OF PLAYING BALL ... STAY HERE AND TAKE A LEAF OUT OF THEIR BOOK!
TAKE A LEAF, TAKE A LEAF! EASY FOR HIM TO SAY!
IS IT MY FAULT IF IT'S TOO SMALL?
?
BUDDY
SPLASH!
554B

A bit stiff

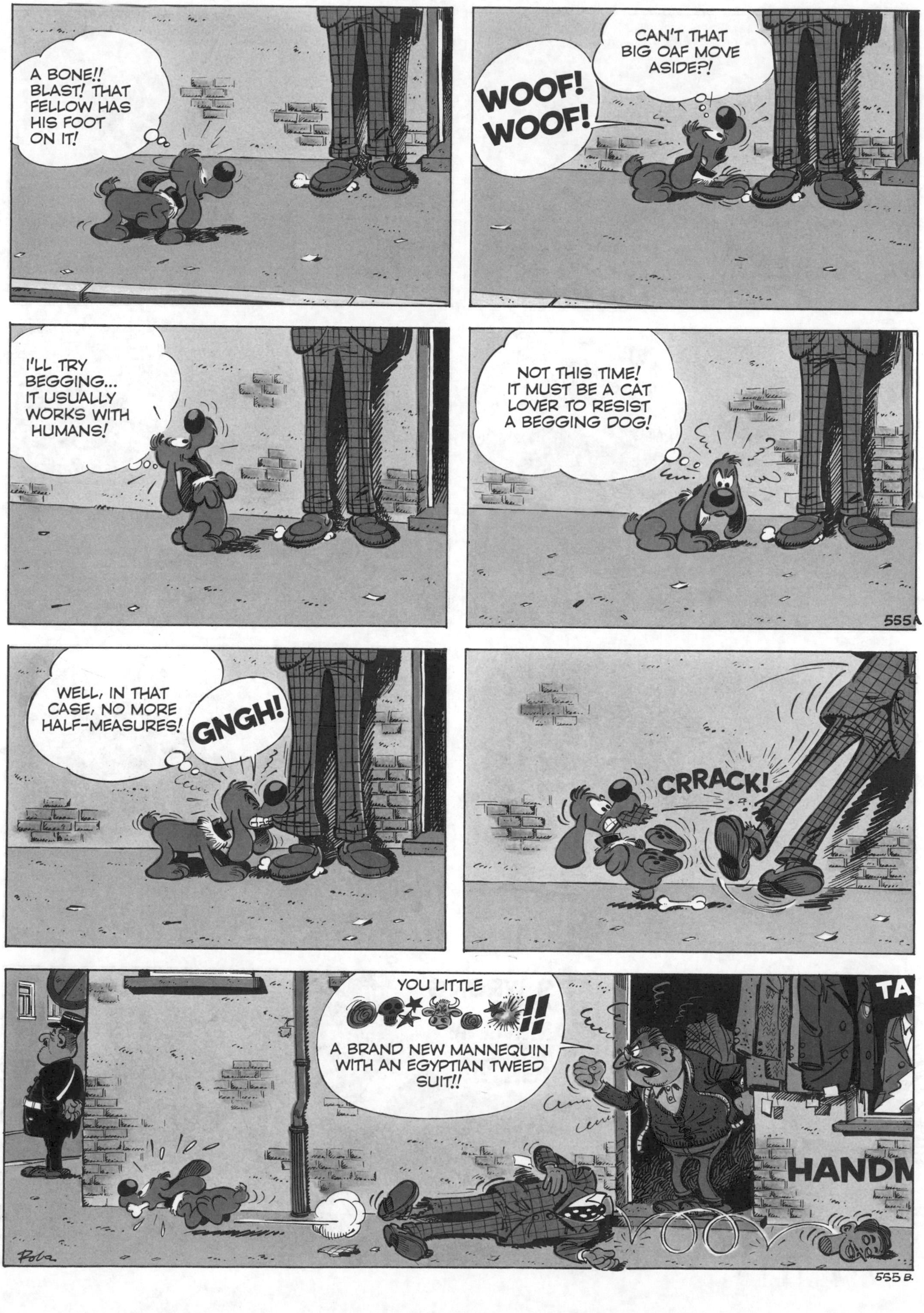
A BONE!! BLAST! THAT FELLOW HAS HIS FOOT ON IT!
CAN'T THAT BIG OAF MOVE ASIDE?!
WOOF! WOOF!
I'LL TRY BEGGING... IT USUALLY WORKS WITH HUMANS!
NOT THIS TIME! IT MUST BE A CAT LOVER TO RESIST A BEGGING DOG!
555A
WELL, IN THAT CASE, NO MORE HALF-MEASURES!
GNGH!
CRRACK!
YOU LITTLE
!!
A BRAND NEW MANNEQUIN WITH AN EGYPTIAN TWEED SUIT!!
TA
HANDM
Roba
555 B.

Nightmare

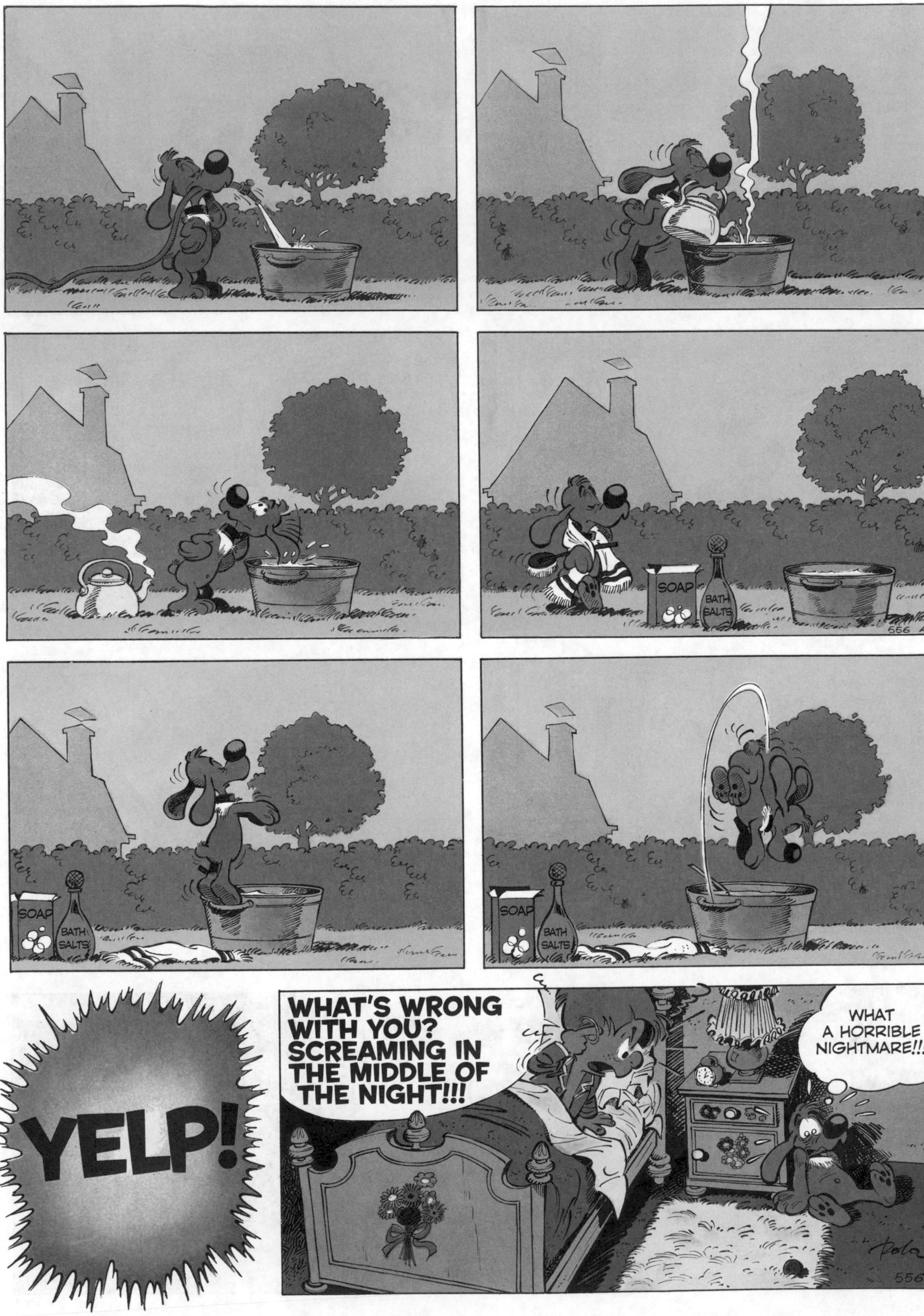
SOAP
BATH SALTS
556 A
SOAP
BATH SALTS
SOAP
BATH SALTS
YELP!
WHAT'S WRONG WITH YOU? SCREAMING IN THE MIDDLE OF THE NIGHT!!!
WHAT A HORRIBLE NIGHTMARE!!!
556 B

Mona Lisa

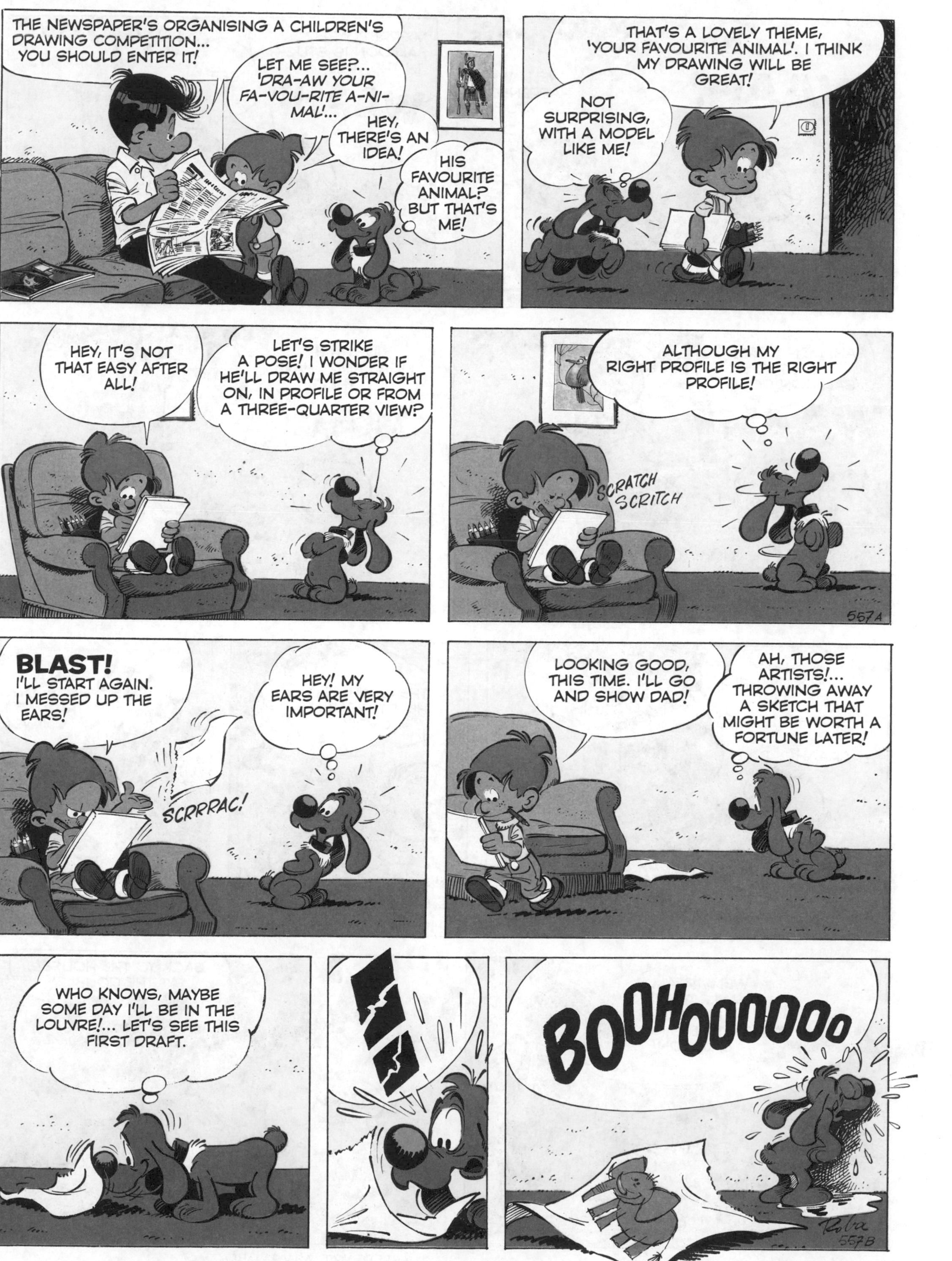

THE NEWSPAPER'S ORGANISING A CHILDREN'S DRAWING COMPETITION... YOU SHOULD ENTER IT!
LET ME SEE?... 'DRA-AW YOUR FA-VOU-RITE A-NI-MAL'...
HEY, THERE'S AN IDEA!
HIS FAVOURITE ANIMAL? BUT THAT'S ME!
THAT'S A LOVELY THEME, 'YOUR FAVOURITE ANIMAL'. I THINK MY DRAWING WILL BE GREAT!
NOT SURPRISING, WITH A MODEL LIKE ME!
HEY, IT'S NOT THAT EASY AFTER ALL!
LET'S STRIKE A POSE! I WONDER IF HE'LL DRAW ME STRAIGHT ON, IN PROFILE OR FROM A THREE-QUARTER VIEW?
ALTHOUGH MY RIGHT PROFILE IS THE RIGHT PROFILE!
SCRATCH SCRITCH
557 A
BLAST! I'LL START AGAIN. I MESSED UP THE EARS!
SCRRRAC!
HEY! MY EARS ARE VERY IMPORTANT!
LOOKING GOOD, THIS TIME. I'LL GO AND SHOW DAD!
AH, THOSE ARTISTS!... THROWING AWAY A SKETCH THAT MIGHT BE WORTH A FORTUNE LATER!
WHO KNOWS, MAYBE SOME DAY I'LL BE IN THE LOUVRE!... LET'S SEE THIS FIRST DRAFT.
BOOHOOOOOOo
Roba
557B

Injustice

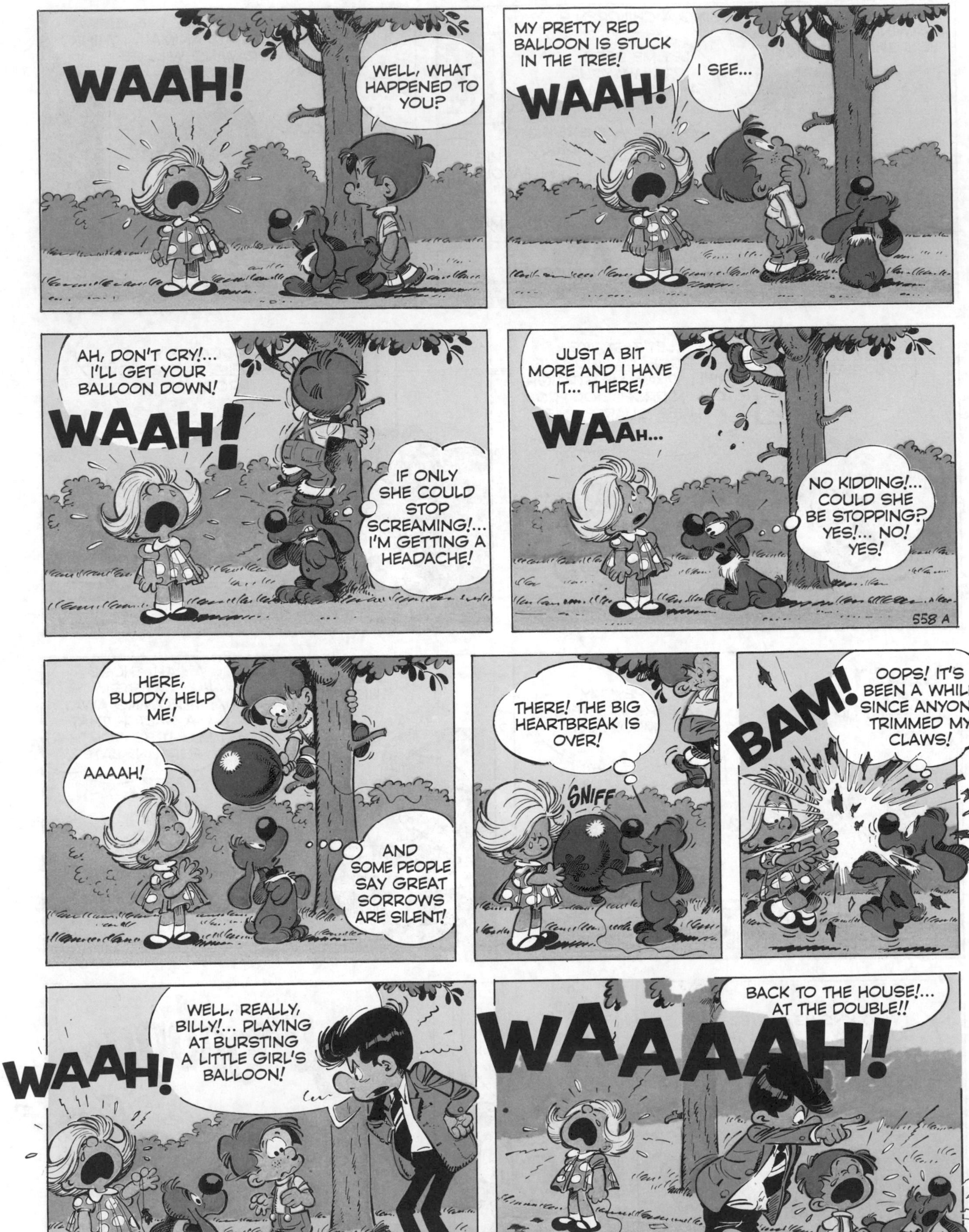
WAAH!
WELL, WHAT HAPPENED TO YOU?
MY PRETTY RED BALLOON IS STUCK IN THE TREE!
WAAH!
I SEE...
AH, DON'T CRY!... I'LL GET YOUR BALLOON DOWN!
WAAH!
IF ONLY SHE COULD STOP SCREAMING!... I'M GETTING A HEADACHE!
JUST A BIT MORE AND I HAVE IT... THERE!
WAAH...
NO KIDDING!... COULD SHE BE STOPPING? YES!... NO! YES!
558 A
HERE, BUDDY, HELP ME!
AAAAH!
AND SOME PEOPLE SAY GREAT SORROWS ARE SILENT!
THERE! THE BIG HEARTBREAK IS OVER!
SNIFF
BAM!
OOPS! IT'S BEEN A WHILE SINCE ANYONE TRIMMED MY CLAWS!
WAAH!
WELL, REALLY, BILLY!... PLAYING AT BURSTING A LITTLE GIRL'S BALLOON!
WAAAAH!
BACK TO THE HOUSE!... AT THE DOUBLE!!
Roba
558 B.

ARTIST'S NOTE: WHAAAAAAHT A GAG!

Time to flea

!
DAD! MUM!
BUT THAT'S TERRIBLE!
IF WHAT YOU SAY IS TRUE, HE'S BETTER OFF OUTSIDE!
YES, HE'S THERE ON THE PAVEMENT!
PEOPLE, WE MUST BE BRAVE AND FACE THE TRUTH: **OUR DOG HAS FLEAS!!**
WE HAVE TO ACT NOW!
559 A
LET'S NOT WASTE TIME! LAUNCH OPERATION 'FLEAS FLEE'!... FOLLOW ME!
SO, ARE YOU WITH ME? WHEN I SAY 'GO', START SATURATION FIRE ALONG A FLANKING MANOEUVRE!
ROGER!
NOW!
?!
BANZAI!
PSSSST
FFFFFT
OPERATION COMPLETED!
WHAT THE?! ARE YOU ALL CRAZY! WHAT WAS THAT ALL ABOUT?!?!... I FIND A WATCH... I SHAKE IT GENTLY TO SEE IF IT WORKS... AND YOU SPRAY ME WITH A WHOLE LOT OF NASTY STUFF!!
Roba 559 B

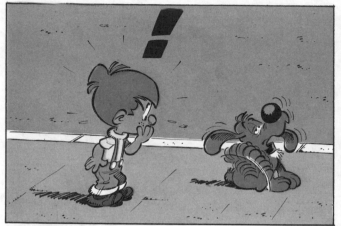

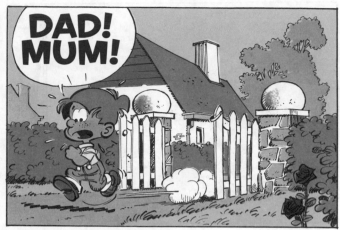

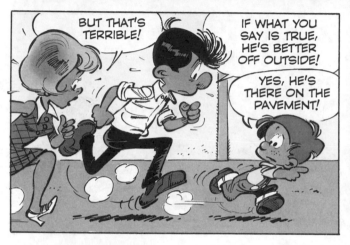

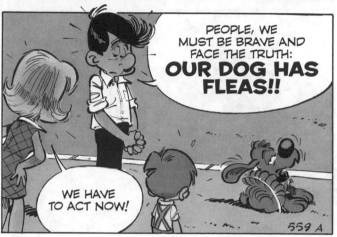

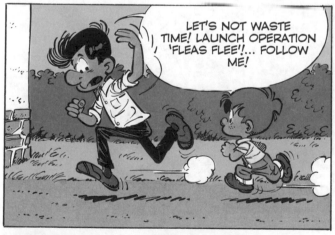

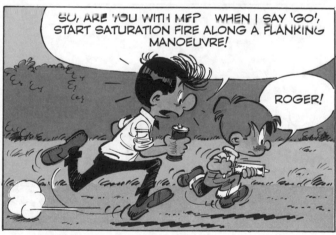

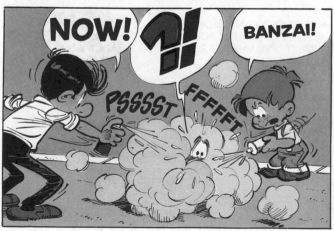

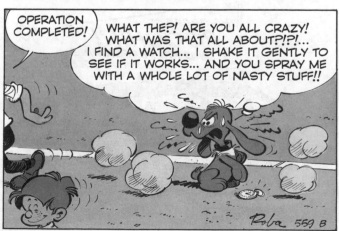

Hitchhiking

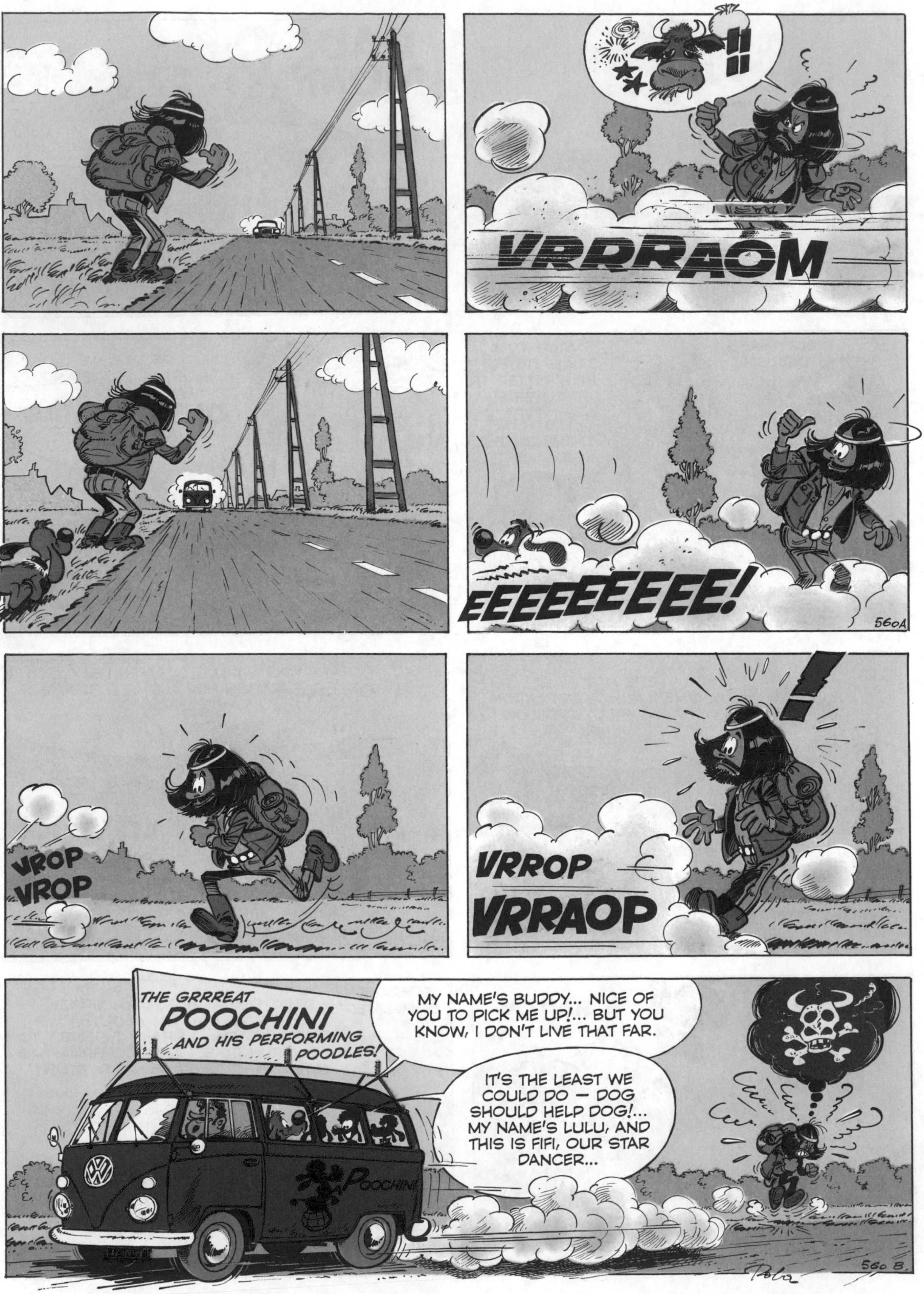
!!
VRRRAOM
EEEEEEEEEE!
560A
VROP
VROP
!
VRROP
VRRAOP
THE GRRREAT
POOCHINI
AND HIS PERFORMING
POODLES!
MY NAME'S BUDDY... NICE OF YOU TO PICK ME UP!... BUT YOU KNOW, I DON'T LIVE THAT FAR.
IT'S THE LEAST WE COULD DO — DOG SHOULD HELP DOG!... MY NAME'S LULU, AND THIS IS FIFI, OUR STAR DANCER...
POOCHINI
560 B.

Pool problems

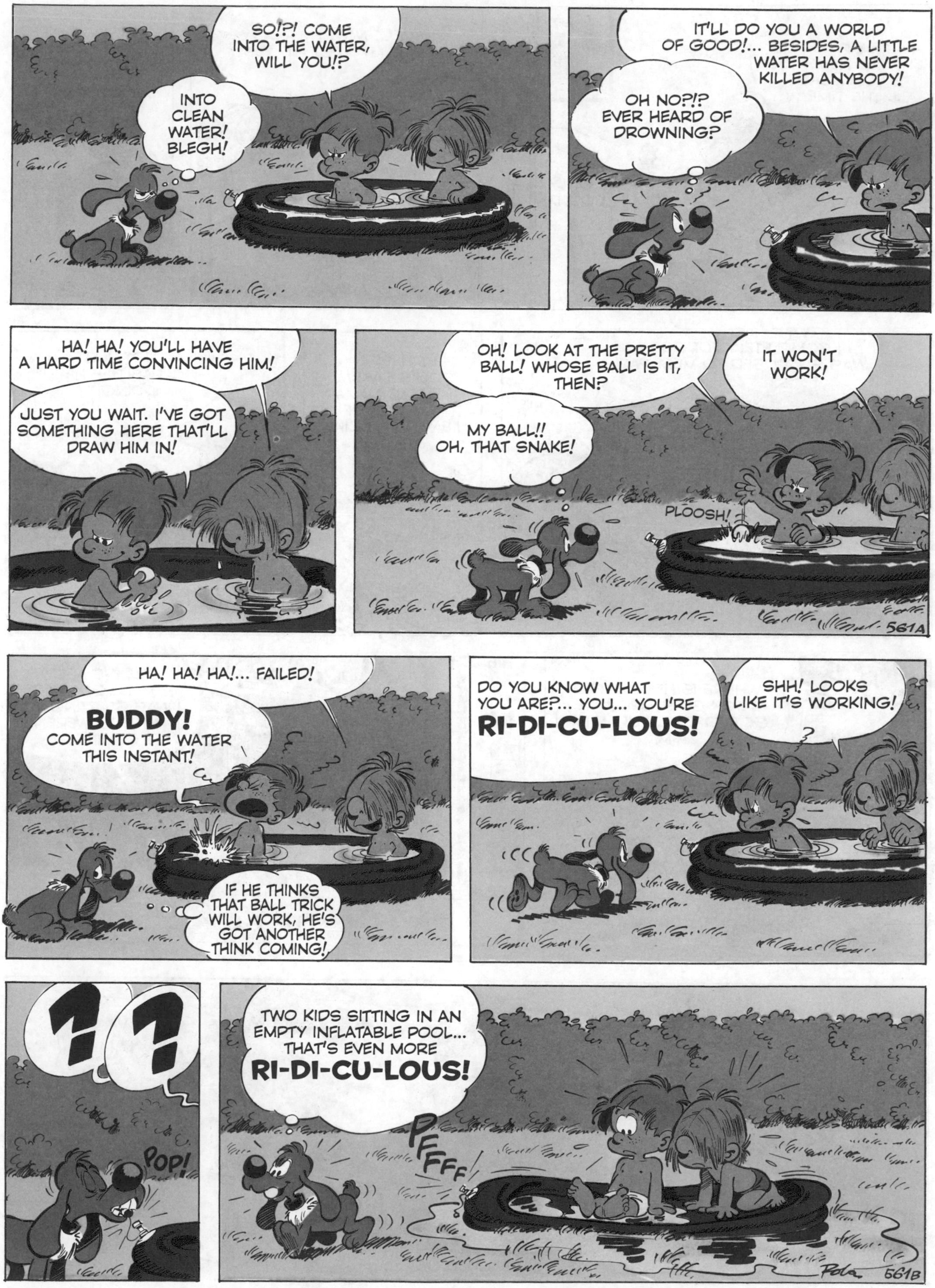

SO!?! COME INTO THE WATER, WILL YOU!?
INTO CLEAN WATER! BLEGH!
IT'LL DO YOU A WORLD OF GOOD!... BESIDES, A LITTLE WATER HAS NEVER KILLED ANYBODY!
OH NO?!? EVER HEARD OF DROWNING?
HA! HA! YOU'LL HAVE A HARD TIME CONVINCING HIM!
JUST YOU WAIT. I'VE GOT SOMETHING HERE THAT'LL DRAW HIM IN!
OH! LOOK AT THE PRETTY BALL! WHOSE BALL IS IT, THEN?
IT WON'T WORK!
MY BALL!! OH, THAT SNAKE!
PLOOSH!
561A
HA! HA! HA!... FAILED!
BUDDY! COME INTO THE WATER THIS INSTANT!
IF HE THINKS THAT BALL TRICK WILL WORK, HE'S GOT ANOTHER THINK COMING!
DO YOU KNOW WHAT YOU ARE?... YOU... YOU'RE RI-DI-CU-LOUS!
SHH! LOOKS LIKE IT'S WORKING!
POP!
TWO KIDS SITTING IN AN EMPTY INFLATABLE POOL... THAT'S EVEN MORE RI-DI-CU-LOUS!
PFFFF
Pola
561B

Bandages

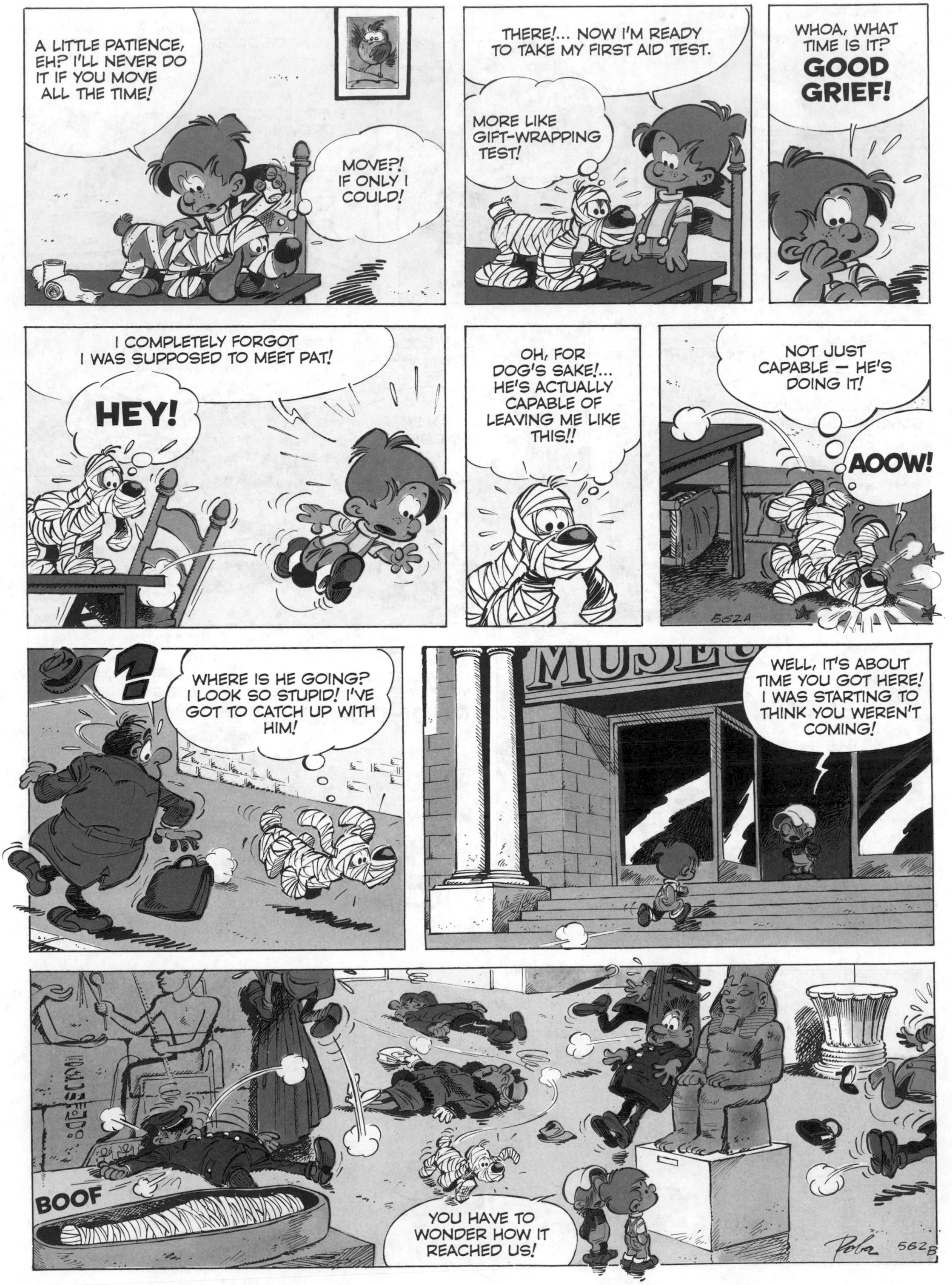

A LITTLE PATIENCE, EH? I'LL NEVER DO IT IF YOU MOVE ALL THE TIME!
MOVE?! IF ONLY I COULD!
THERE!... NOW I'M READY TO TAKE MY FIRST AID TEST.
MORE LIKE GIFT-WRAPPING TEST!
WHOA, WHAT TIME IS IT? GOOD GRIEF!
I COMPLETELY FORGOT I WAS SUPPOSED TO MEET PAT!
HEY!
OH, FOR DOG'S SAKE!... HE'S ACTUALLY CAPABLE OF LEAVING ME LIKE THIS!!
NOT JUST CAPABLE — HE'S DOING IT!
AOOW!
?
WHERE IS HE GOING? I LOOK SO STUPID! I'VE GOT TO CATCH UP WITH HIM!
MUSEU
WELL, IT'S ABOUT TIME YOU GOT HERE! I WAS STARTING TO THINK YOU WEREN'T COMING!
BOOF
YOU HAVE TO WONDER HOW IT REACHED US!
Roba
562B

Ahh, girls!

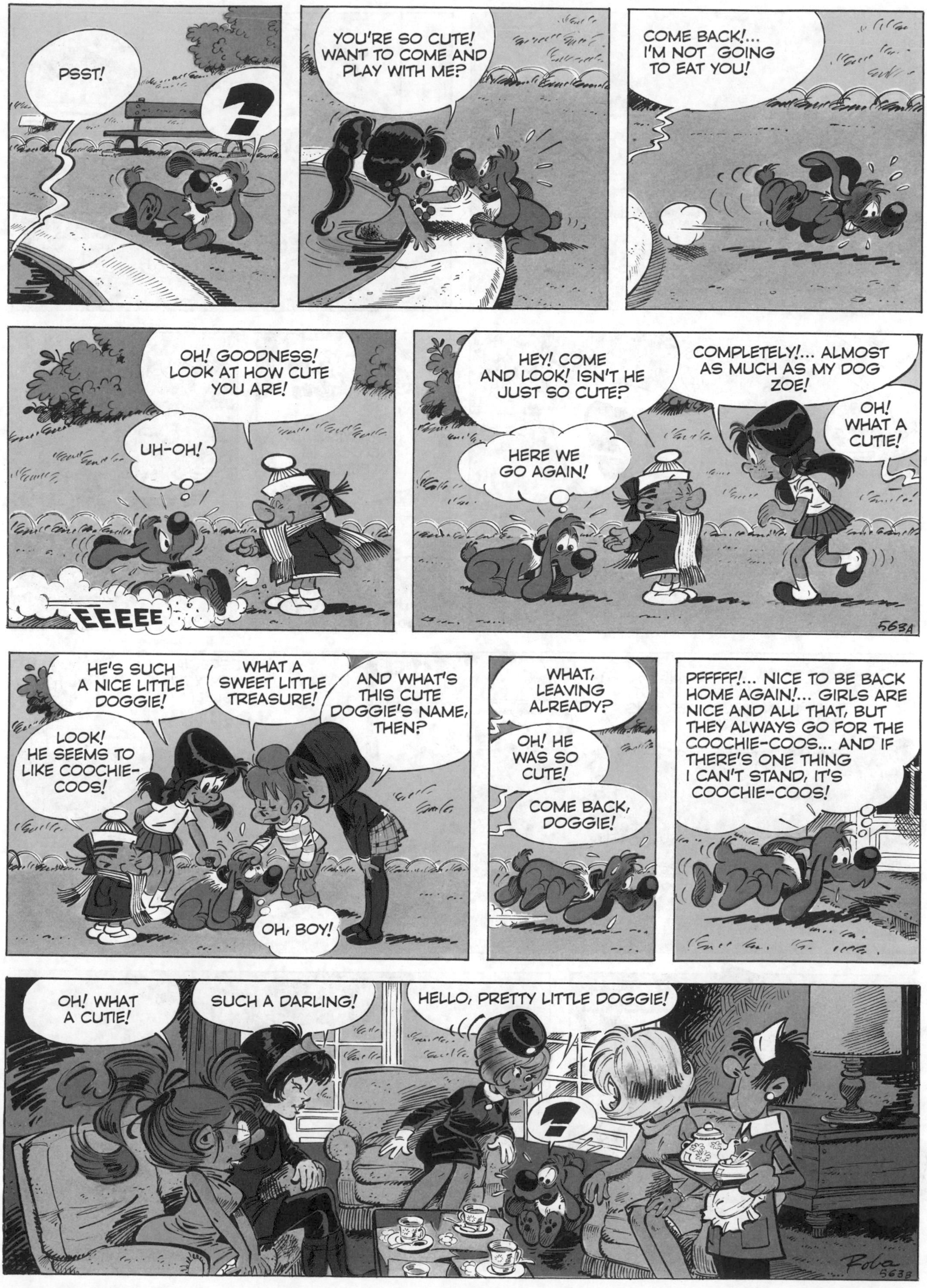

PSST!
YOU'RE SO CUTE! WANT TO COME AND PLAY WITH ME?
COME BACK!... I'M NOT GOING TO EAT YOU!
OH! GOODNESS! LOOK AT HOW CUTE YOU ARE!
UH-OH!
EEEEE
HEY! COME AND LOOK! ISN'T HE JUST SO CUTE?
HERE WE GO AGAIN!
COMPLETELY!... ALMOST AS MUCH AS MY DOG ZOE!
OH! WHAT A CUTIE!
563A
HE'S SUCH A NICE LITTLE DOGGIE!
WHAT A SWEET LITTLE TREASURE!
AND WHAT'S THIS CUTE DOGGIE'S NAME, THEN?
LOOK! HE SEEMS TO LIKE COOCHIE-COOS!
OH, BOY!
WHAT, LEAVING ALREADY?
OH! HE WAS SO CUTE!
COME BACK, DOGGIE!
PFFFFF!... NICE TO BE BACK HOME AGAIN!... GIRLS ARE NICE AND ALL THAT, BUT THEY ALWAYS GO FOR THE COOCHIE-COOS... AND IF THERE'S ONE THING I CAN'T STAND, IT'S COOCHIE-COOS!
OH! WHAT A CUTIE!
SUCH A DARLING!
HELLO, PRETTY LITTLE DOGGIE!
Roba
563B

Hedge-hopping

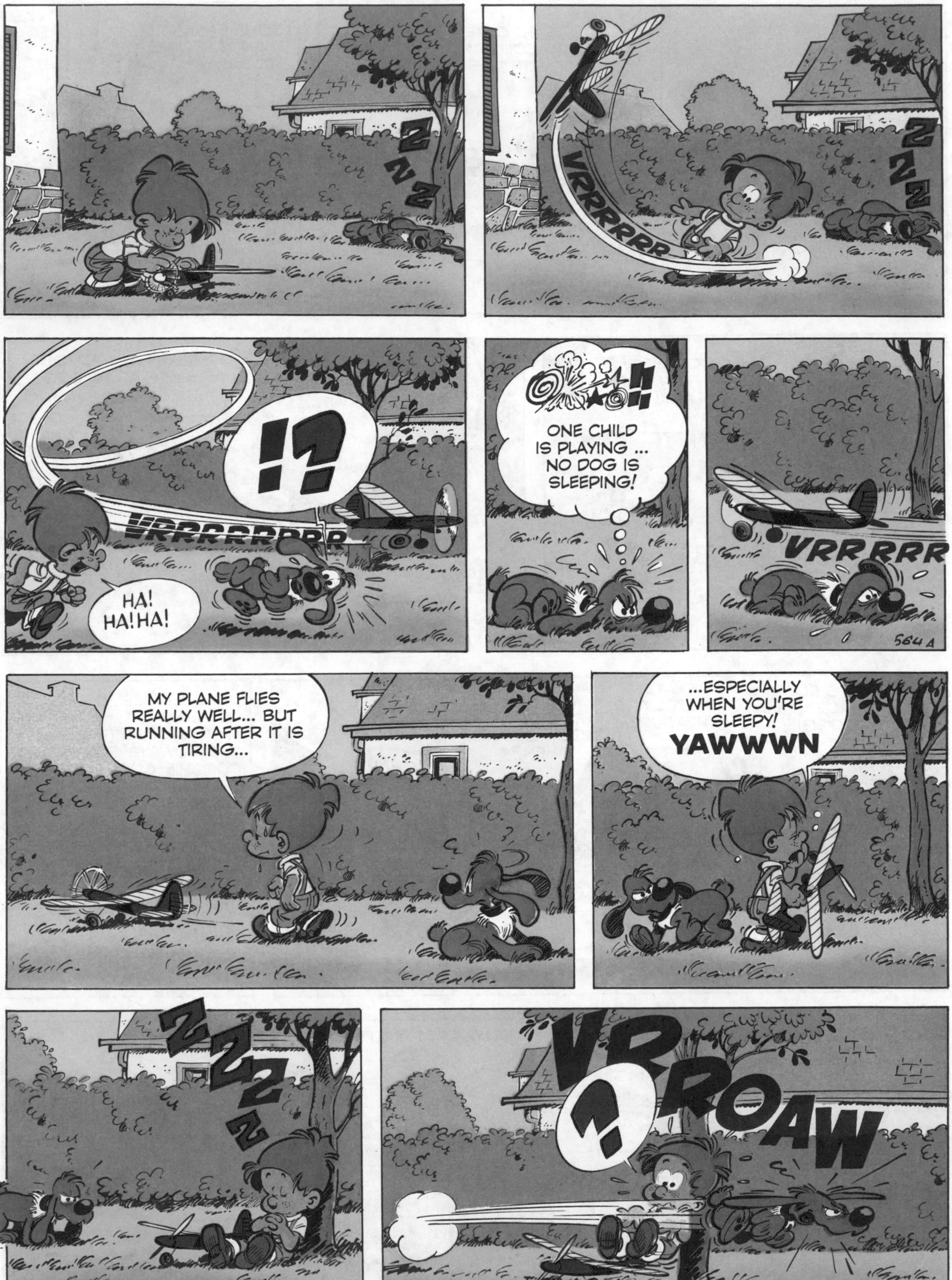
ZZZ
VRRRRRRR
ZZZ
!?
VRRRRRRRRR
HA! HA! HA!
ONE CHILD IS PLAYING ... NO DOG IS SLEEPING!
VRRRRR
564A
MY PLANE FLIES REALLY WELL... BUT RUNNING AFTER IT IS TIRING...
...ESPECIALLY WHEN YOU'RE SLEEPY!
YAWWWN
ZZZZ
VRROAW
?
Roba 564B

Nice try!

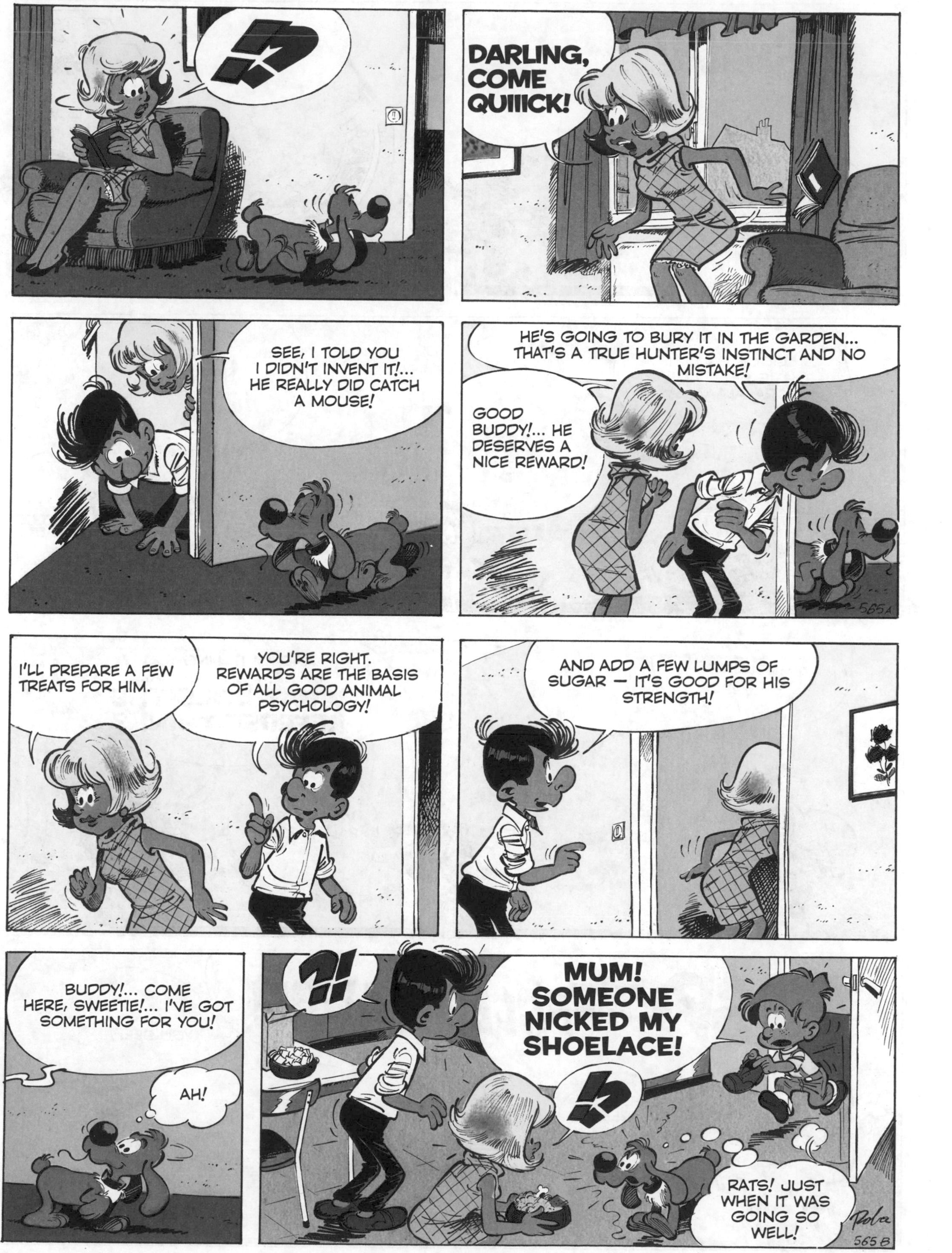

DARLING, COME QUIIICK!
SEE, I TOLD YOU I DIDN'T INVENT IT!... HE REALLY DID CATCH A MOUSE!
HE'S GOING TO BURY IT IN THE GARDEN... THAT'S A TRUE HUNTER'S INSTINCT AND NO MISTAKE!
GOOD BUDDY!... HE DESERVES A NICE REWARD!
565 A
I'LL PREPARE A FEW TREATS FOR HIM.
YOU'RE RIGHT. REWARDS ARE THE BASIS OF ALL GOOD ANIMAL PSYCHOLOGY!
AND ADD A FEW LUMPS OF SUGAR — IT'S GOOD FOR HIS STRENGTH!
BUDDY!... COME HERE, SWEETIE!... I'VE GOT SOMETHING FOR YOU!
AH!
MUM! SOMEONE NICKED MY SHOELACE!
RATS! JUST WHEN IT WAS GOING SO WELL!
Roba
565 B

Ping-pong

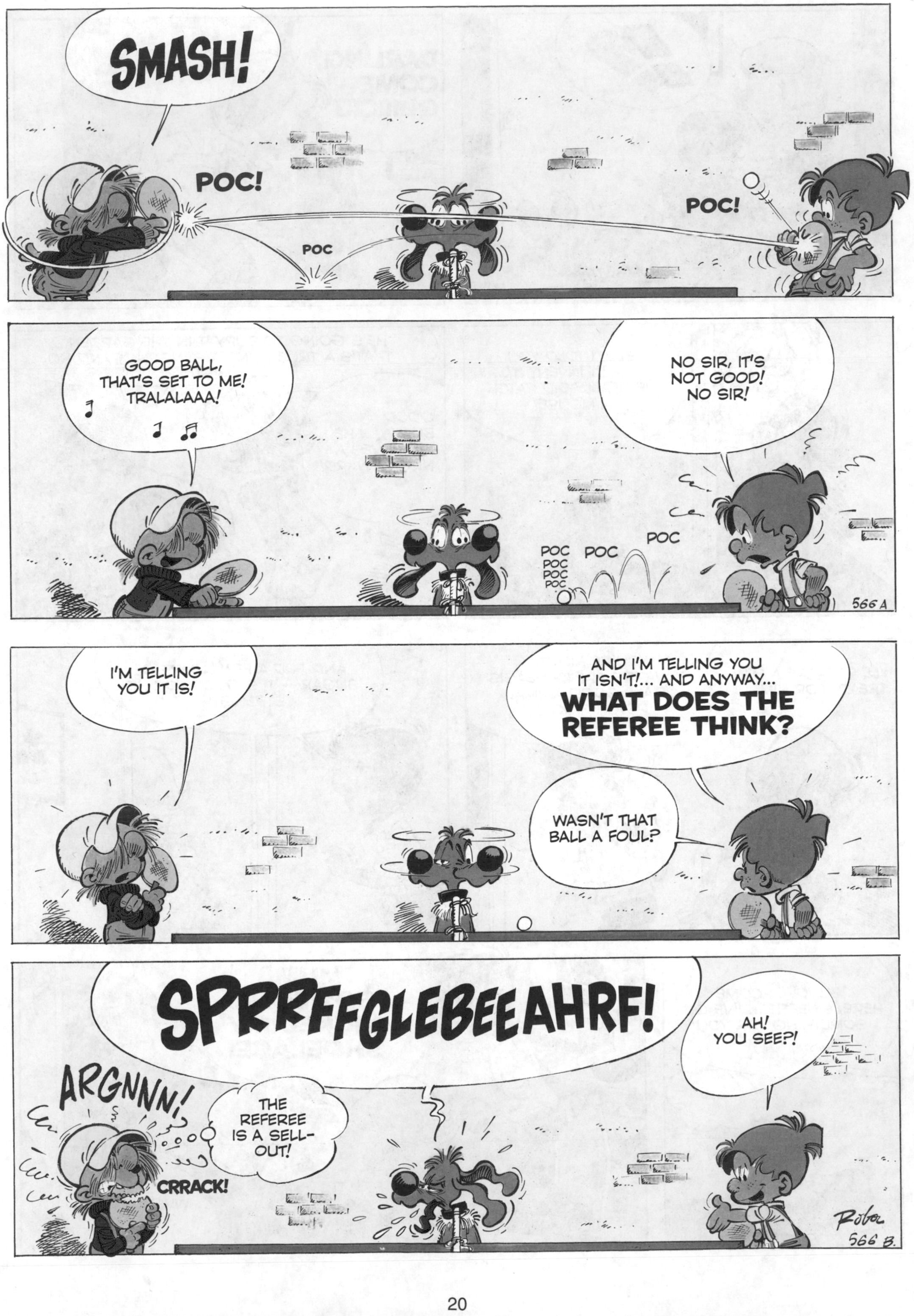
SMASH!
POC!
POC
POC!
GOOD BALL, THAT'S SET TO ME! TRALALAAA!
NO SIR, IT'S NOT GOOD! NO SIR!
POC POC POC POC
POC
POC
566 A
I'M TELLING YOU IT IS!
AND I'M TELLING YOU IT ISN'T!... AND ANYWAY... WHAT DOES THE REFEREE THINK?
WASN'T THAT BALL A FOUL?
SPRRFFGLEBEEAHRF!
AH! YOU SEE?!
ARGNNN!
THE REFEREE IS A SELL-OUT!
CRRACK!
Roba
566 B.

Falls

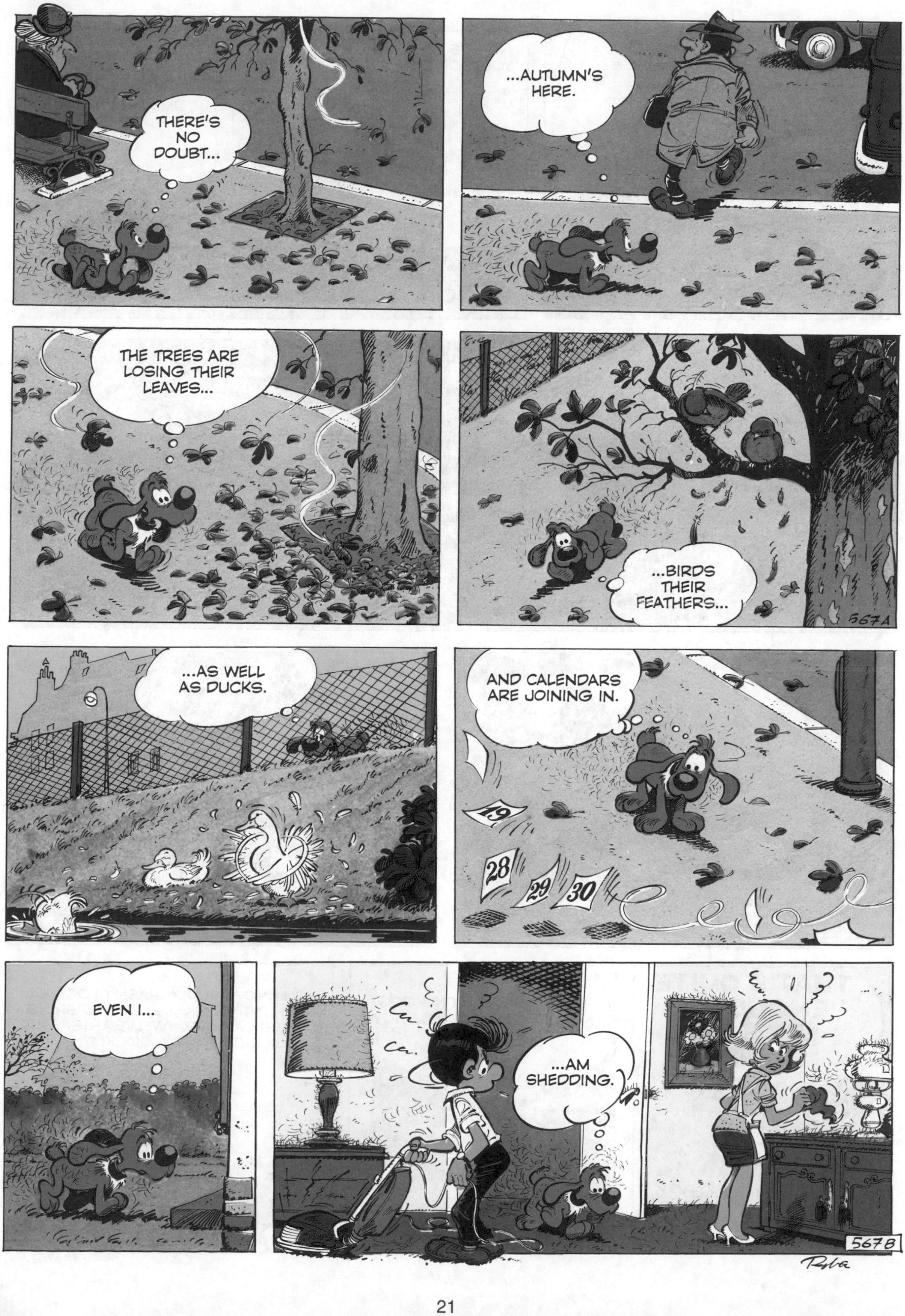
THERE'S NO DOUBT...
...AUTUMN'S HERE.
THE TREES ARE LOSING THEIR LEAVES...
...BIRDS THEIR FEATHERS...
567A
...AS WELL AS DUCKS.
AND CALENDARS ARE JOINING IN.
19
28
29
30
EVEN I...
...AM SHEDDING.
567B
Roba

Hunting trophies

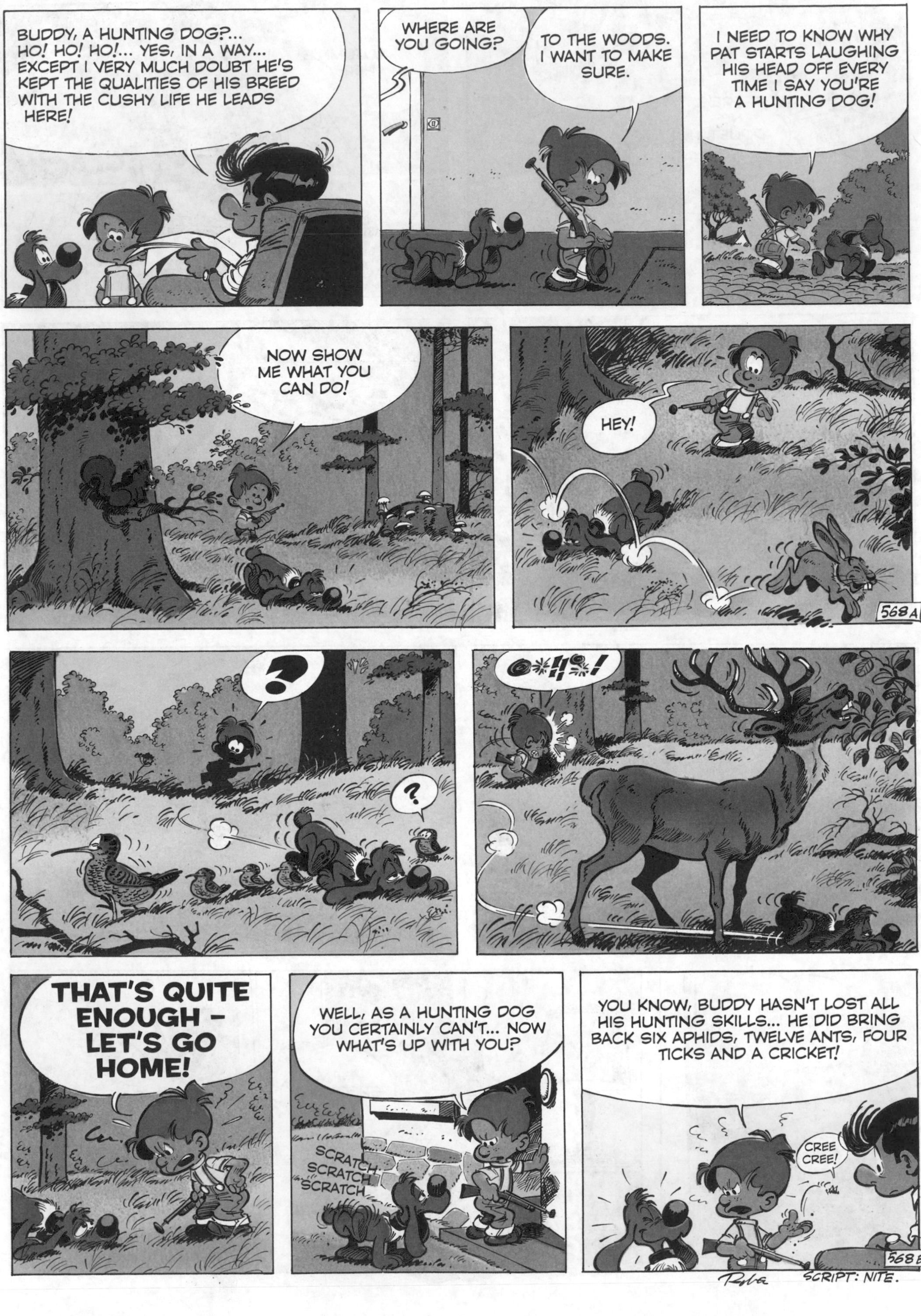
BUDDY, A HUNTING DOG?... HO! HO! HO!... YES, IN A WAY... EXCEPT I VERY MUCH DOUBT HE'S KEPT THE QUALITIES OF HIS BREED WITH THE CUSHY LIFE HE LEADS HERE!
WHERE ARE YOU GOING?
TO THE WOODS. I WANT TO MAKE SURE.
I NEED TO KNOW WHY PAT STARTS LAUGHING HIS HEAD OFF EVERY TIME I SAY YOU'RE A HUNTING DOG!
NOW SHOW ME WHAT YOU CAN DO!
HEY!
568 A
?
?
THAT'S QUITE ENOUGH – LET'S GO HOME!
WELL, AS A HUNTING DOG YOU CERTAINLY CAN'T... NOW WHAT'S UP WITH YOU?
SCRATCH
SCRATCH
SCRATCH
YOU KNOW, BUDDY HASN'T LOST ALL HIS HUNTING SKILLS... HE DID BRING BACK SIX APHIDS, TWELVE ANTS, FOUR TICKS AND A CRICKET!
CREE CREE!
568 B
Roba
SCRIPT: NITE.

Hot dog rod

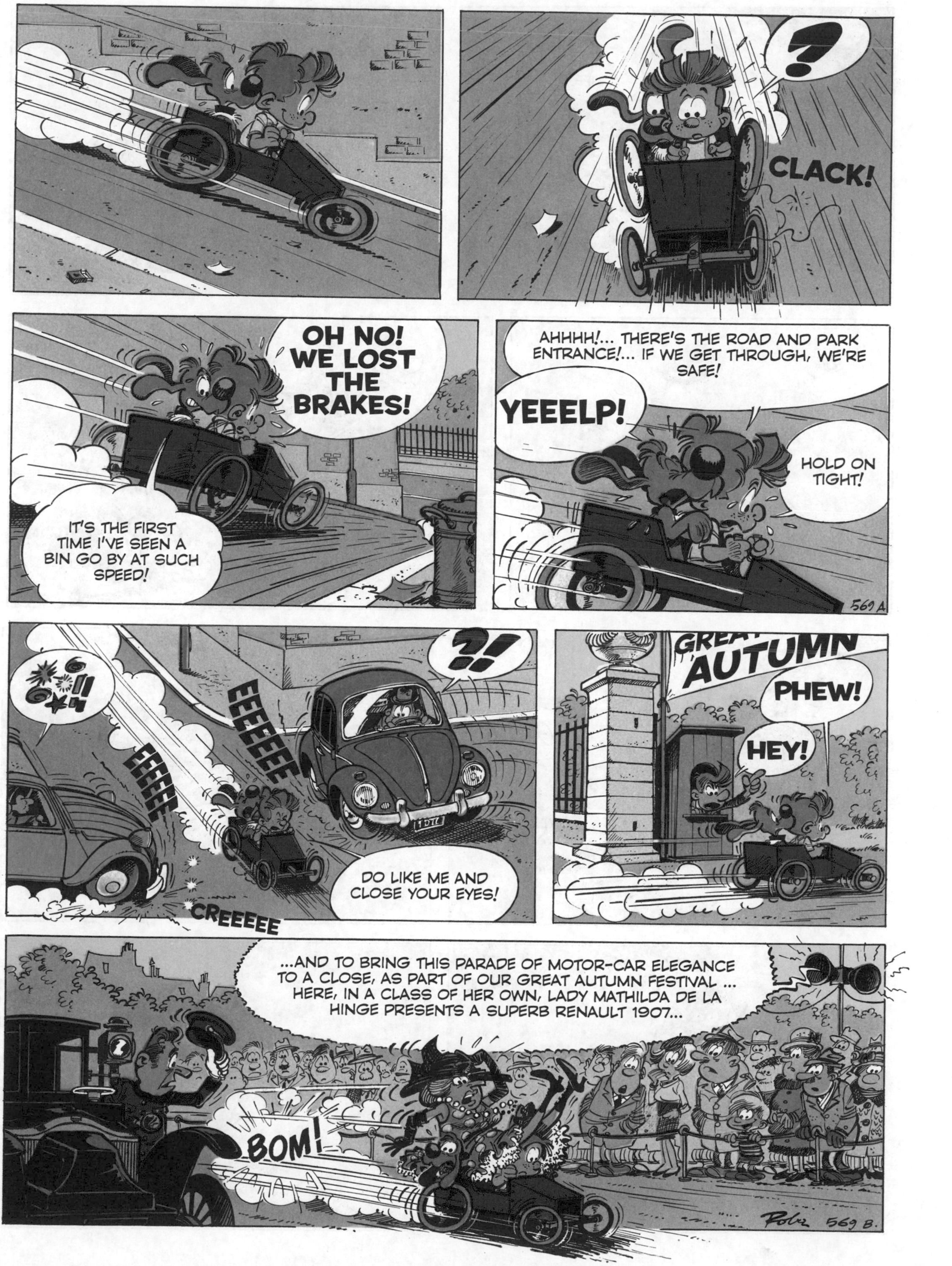

?
CLACK!
OH NO! WE LOST THE BRAKES!
IT'S THE FIRST TIME I'VE SEEN A BIN GO BY AT SUCH SPEED!
AHHHH!... THERE'S THE ROAD AND PARK ENTRANCE!... IF WE GET THROUGH, WE'RE SAFE!
YEEELP!
HOLD ON TIGHT!
569 A
EEEEEEE
EEEEEE
?!
DO LIKE ME AND CLOSE YOUR EYES!
CREEEEE
AUTUMN
PHEW!
HEY!
...AND TO BRING THIS PARADE OF MOTOR-CAR ELEGANCE TO A CLOSE, AS PART OF OUR GREAT AUTUMN FESTIVAL ... HERE, IN A CLASS OF HER OWN, LADY MATHILDA DE LA HINGE PRESENTS A SUPERB RENAULT 1907...
BOM!
Roba 569 B.

On guard...

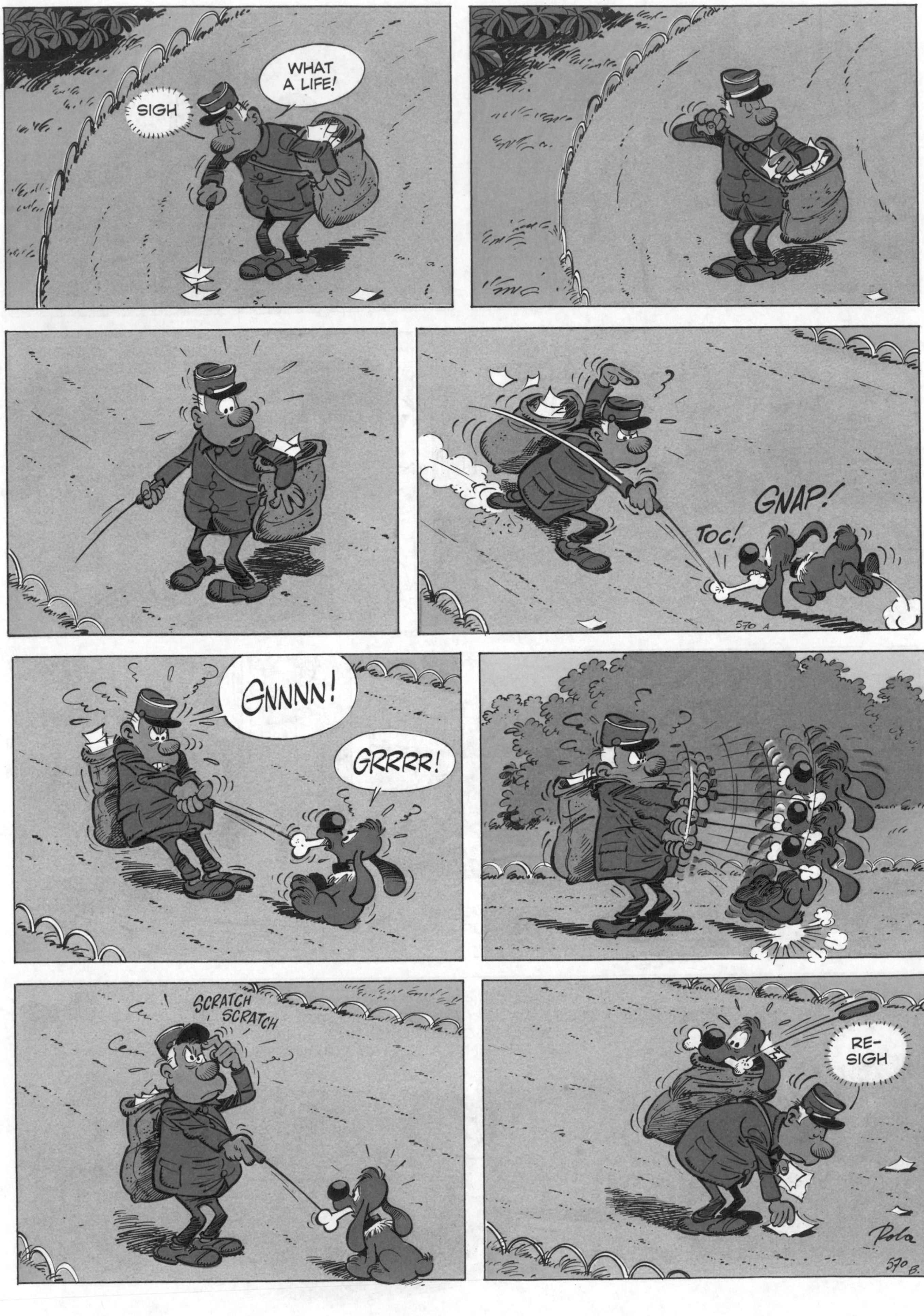
SIGH
WHAT A LIFE!
GNAP!
TOC!
570 A
GNNNN!
GRRRR!
SCRATCH SCRATCH
RE-SIGH
Rola
570 B.

First snowflakes

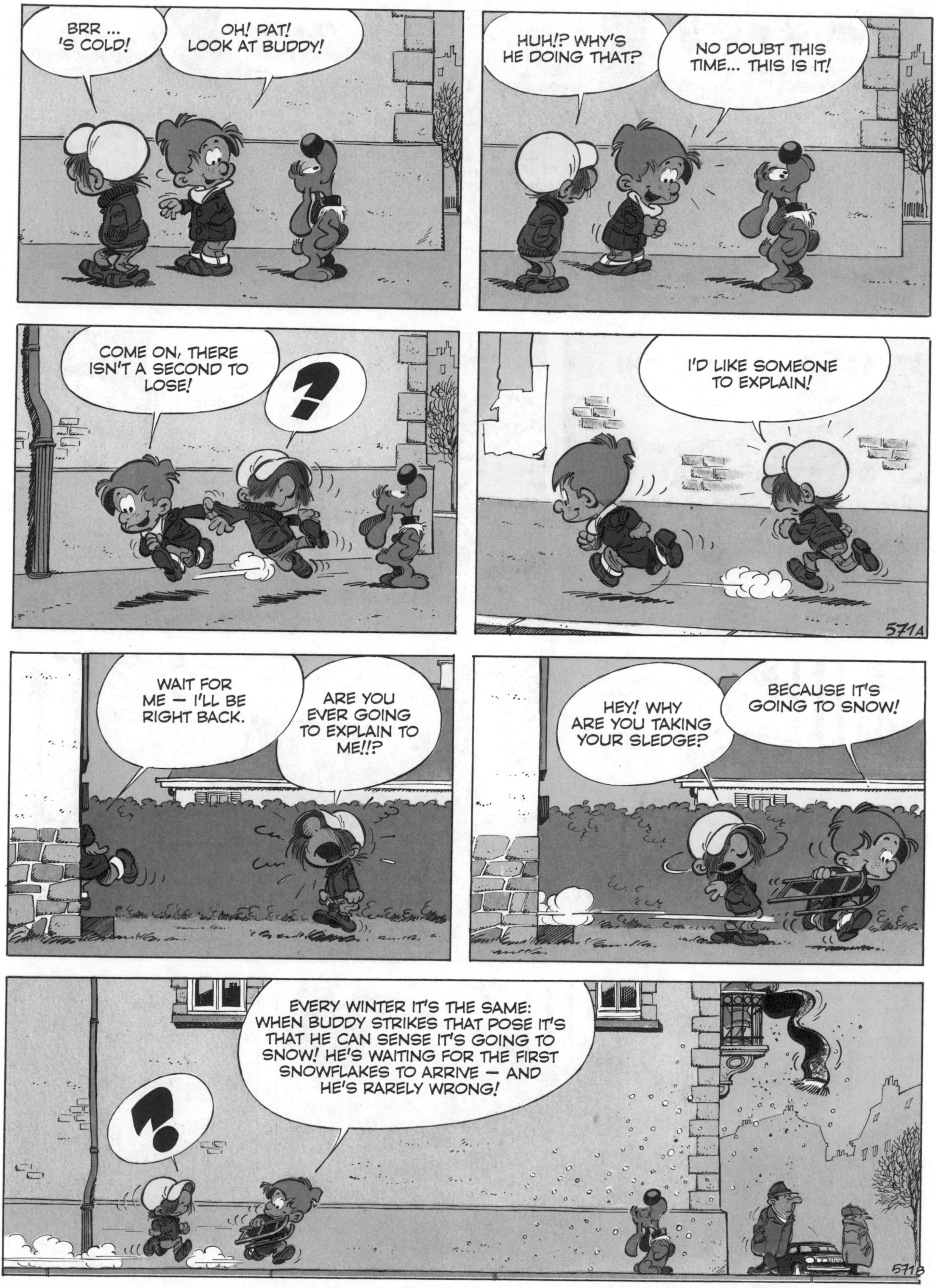
BRR ... 'S COLD!
OH! PAT! LOOK AT BUDDY!
HUH!? WHY'S HE DOING THAT?
NO DOUBT THIS TIME... THIS IS IT!
COME ON, THERE ISN'T A SECOND TO LOSE!
?
I'D LIKE SOMEONE TO EXPLAIN!
571A
WAIT FOR ME — I'LL BE RIGHT BACK.
ARE YOU EVER GOING TO EXPLAIN TO ME!!?
HEY! WHY ARE YOU TAKING YOUR SLEDGE?
BECAUSE IT'S GOING TO SNOW!
?
EVERY WINTER IT'S THE SAME: WHEN BUDDY STRIKES THAT POSE IT'S THAT HE CAN SENSE IT'S GOING TO SNOW! HE'S WAITING FOR THE FIRST SNOWFLAKES TO ARRIVE — AND HE'S RARELY WRONG!
571B

Slippery business

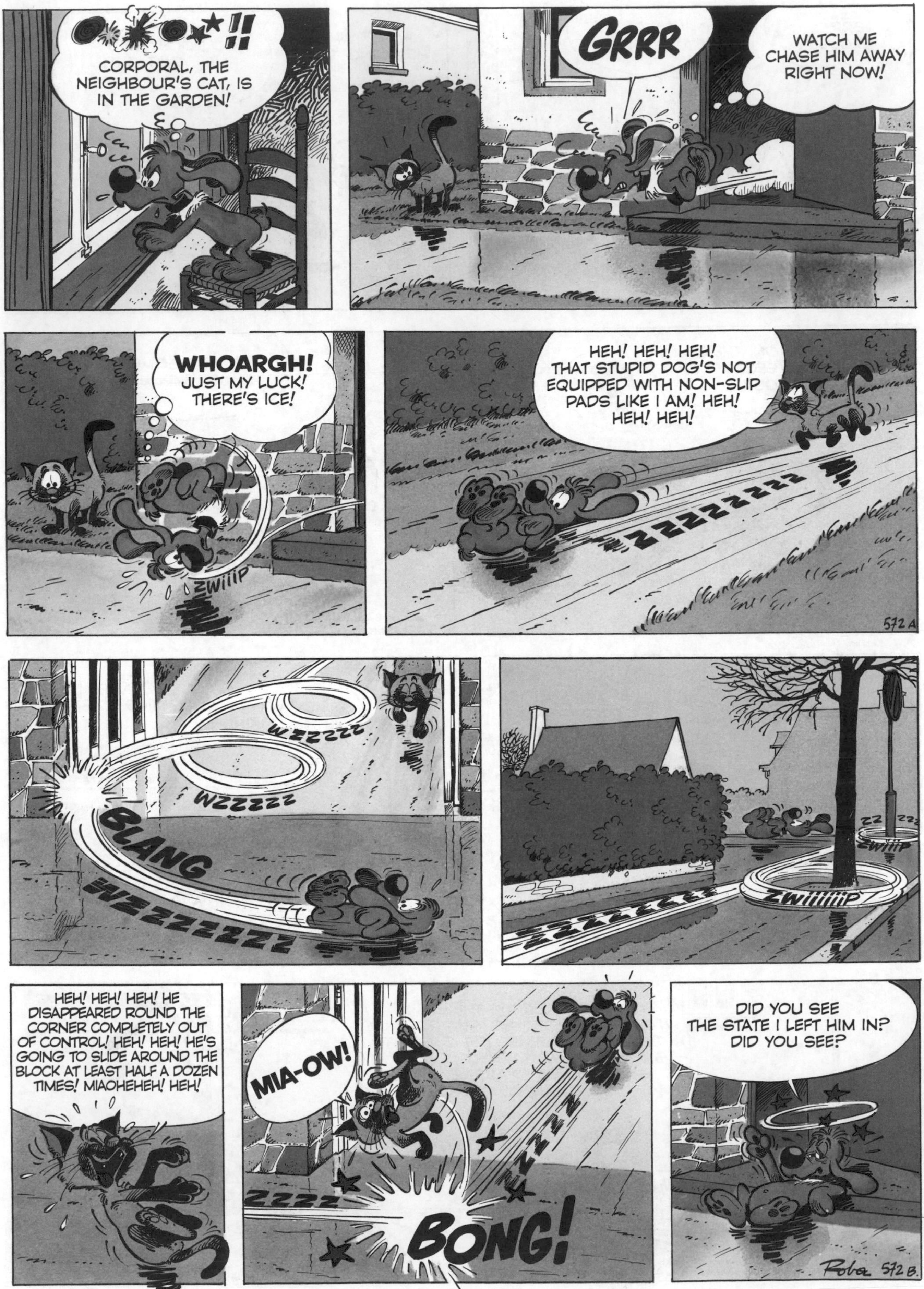

CORPORAL, THE NEIGHBOUR'S CAT, IS IN THE GARDEN!
GRRR
WATCH ME CHASE HIM AWAY RIGHT NOW!
WHOARGH! JUST MY LUCK! THERE'S ICE!
ZWIIIP
HEH! HEH! HEH! THAT STUPID DOG'S NOT EQUIPPED WITH NON-SLIP PADS LIKE I AM! HEH! HEH! HEH!
ZZZZZZZZZ
572 A
WZZZZZ
WZZZZZ
BLANG
WZZZZZZZZ
ZWIIIP
ZWIIIIIIP
HEH! HEH! HEH! HE DISAPPEARED ROUND THE CORNER COMPLETELY OUT OF CONTROL! HEH! HEH! HE'S GOING TO SLIDE AROUND THE BLOCK AT LEAST HALF A DOZEN TIMES! MIAOHEHEH! HEH!
MIA-OW!
ZZZZ
BONG!
DID YOU SEE THE STATE I LEFT HIM IN? DID YOU SEE?
Roba 572 B.

Weather forecast

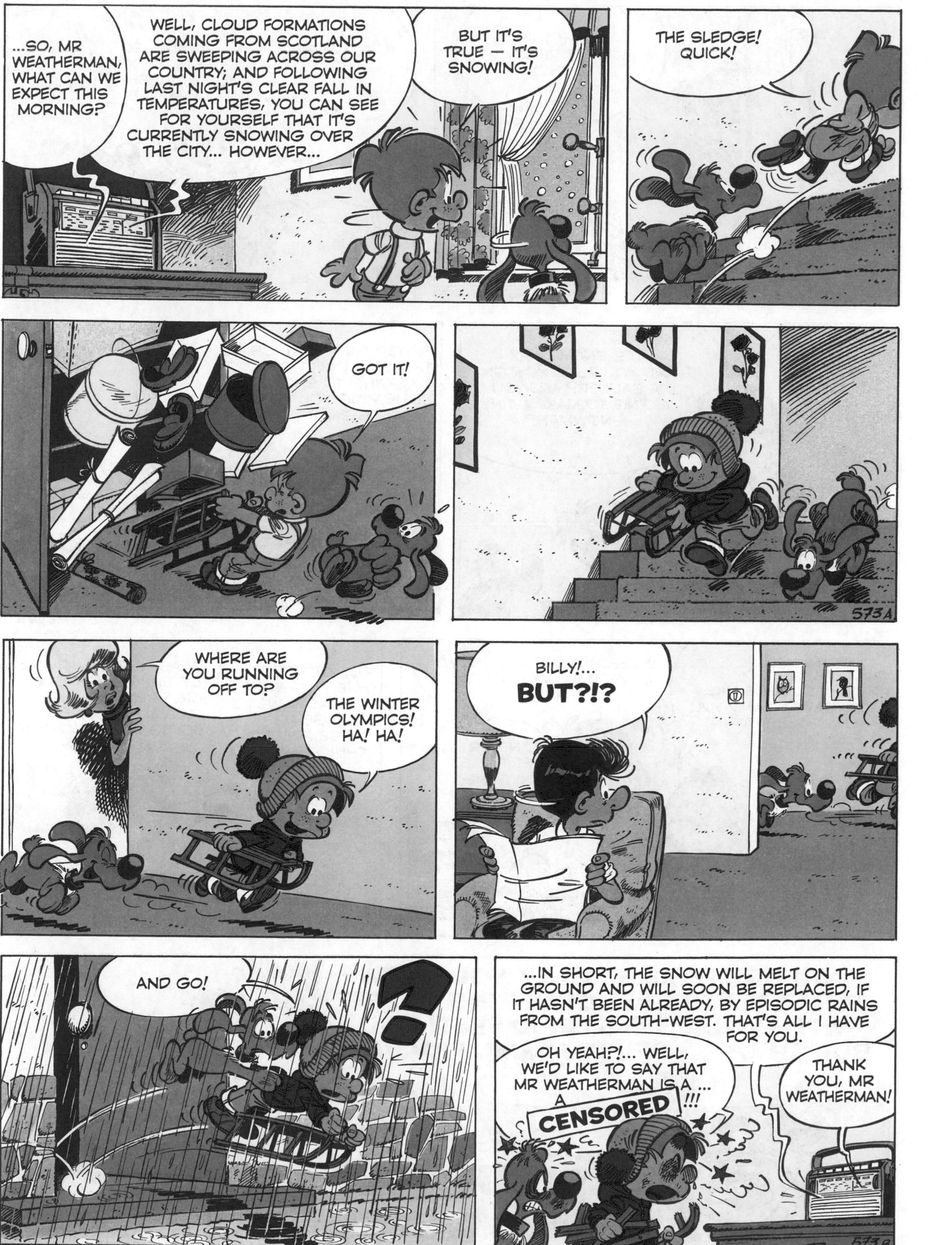

...SO, MR WEATHERMAN, WHAT CAN WE EXPECT THIS MORNING?
WELL, CLOUD FORMATIONS COMING FROM SCOTLAND ARE SWEEPING ACROSS OUR COUNTRY; AND FOLLOWING LAST NIGHT'S CLEAR FALL IN TEMPERATURES, YOU CAN SEE FOR YOURSELF THAT IT'S CURRENTLY SNOWING OVER THE CITY... HOWEVER...
BUT IT'S TRUE — IT'S SNOWING!
THE SLEDGE! QUICK!
GOT IT!
573A
WHERE ARE YOU RUNNING OFF TO?
THE WINTER OLYMPICS! HA! HA!
BILLY!... BUT?!?
AND GO!
...IN SHORT, THE SNOW WILL MELT ON THE GROUND AND WILL SOON BE REPLACED, IF IT HASN'T BEEN ALREADY, BY EPISODIC RAINS FROM THE SOUTH-WEST. THAT'S ALL I HAVE FOR YOU.
OH YEAH?!... WELL, WE'D LIKE TO SAY THAT MR WEATHERMAN IS A ... A CENSORED !!!
THANK YOU, MR WEATHERMAN!
573B

Crystals

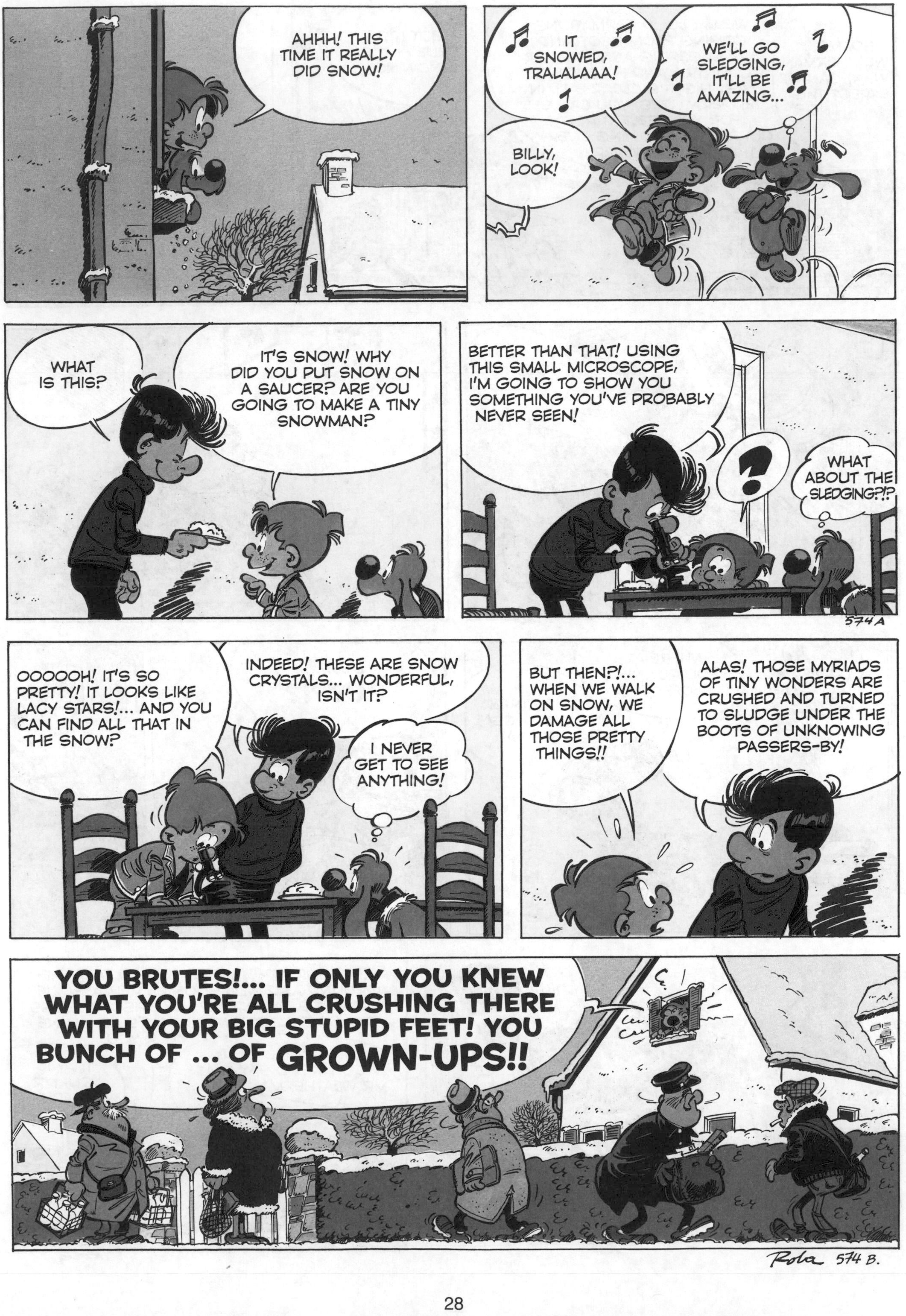
AHHH! THIS TIME IT REALLY DID SNOW!
IT SNOWED, TRALALAAA!
WE'LL GO SLEDGING, IT'LL BE AMAZING...
BILLY, LOOK!
WHAT IS THIS?
IT'S SNOW! WHY DID YOU PUT SNOW ON A SAUCER? ARE YOU GOING TO MAKE A TINY SNOWMAN?
BETTER THAN THAT! USING THIS SMALL MICROSCOPE, I'M GOING TO SHOW YOU SOMETHING YOU'VE PROBABLY NEVER SEEN!
?
WHAT ABOUT THE SLEDGING?!?
574 A
OOOOOH! IT'S SO PRETTY! IT LOOKS LIKE LACY STARS!... AND YOU CAN FIND ALL THAT IN THE SNOW?
INDEED! THESE ARE SNOW CRYSTALS... WONDERFUL, ISN'T IT?
I NEVER GET TO SEE ANYTHING!
BUT THEN?!... WHEN WE WALK ON SNOW, WE DAMAGE ALL THOSE PRETTY THINGS!!
ALAS! THOSE MYRIADS OF TINY WONDERS ARE CRUSHED AND TURNED TO SLUDGE UNDER THE BOOTS OF UNKNOWING PASSERS-BY!
YOU BRUTES!... IF ONLY YOU KNEW WHAT YOU'RE ALL CRUSHING THERE WITH YOUR BIG STUPID FEET! YOU BUNCH OF ... OF GROWN-UPS!!
Roba 574 B.

There are balls … and balls

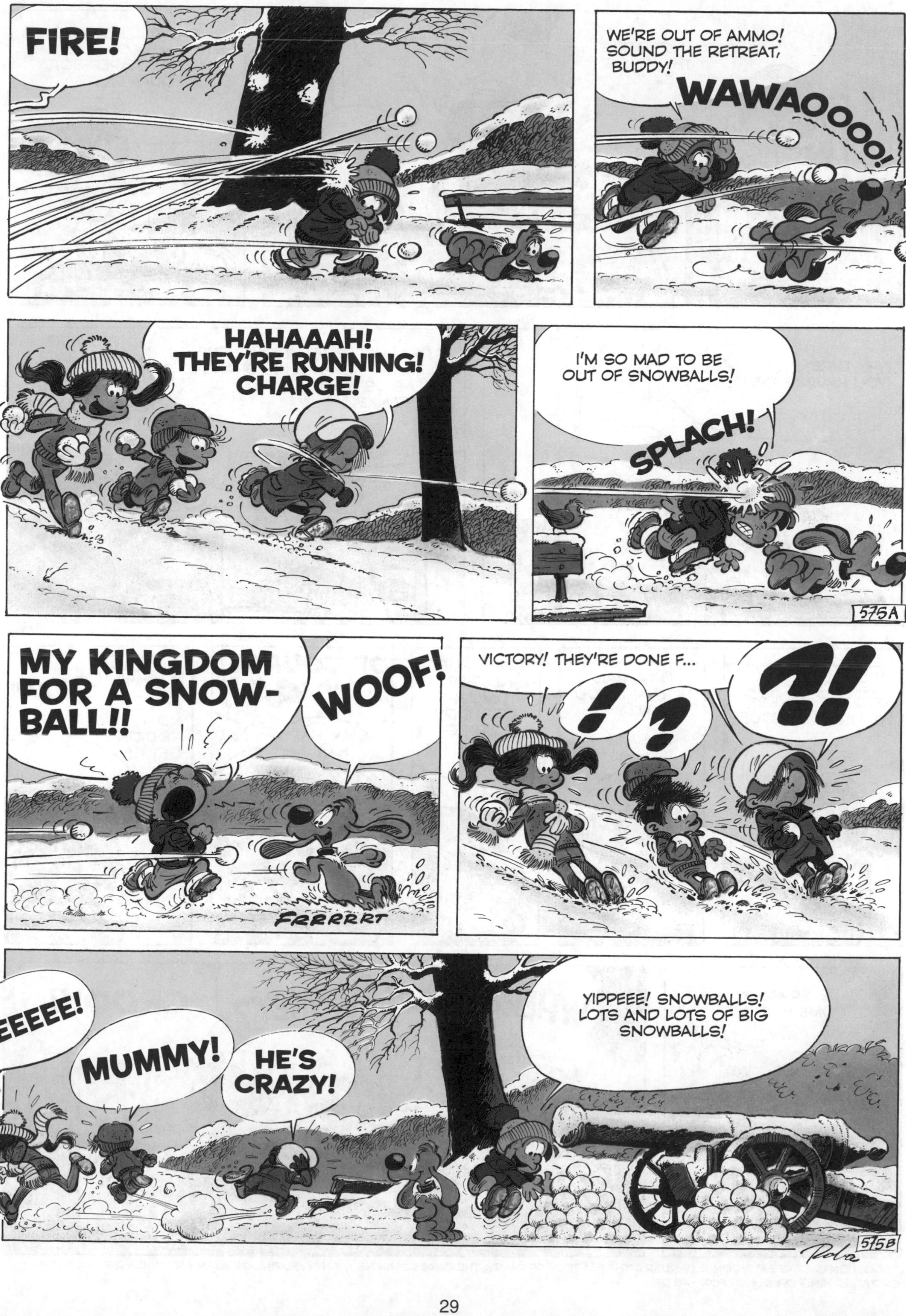
FIRE!
WE'RE OUT OF AMMO! SOUND THE RETREAT, BUDDY!
WAWAOOOO!
HAHAAAH! THEY'RE RUNNING! CHARGE!
I'M SO MAD TO BE OUT OF SNOWBALLS!
SPLACH!
575A
MY KINGDOM FOR A SNOW-BALL!!
WOOF!
FRRRRRT
VICTORY! THEY'RE DONE F...
!
?
?!
EEEEEEE!
MUMMY!
HE'S CRAZY!
YIPPEEE! SNOWBALLS! LOTS AND LOTS OF BIG SNOWBALLS!
575B
Roba

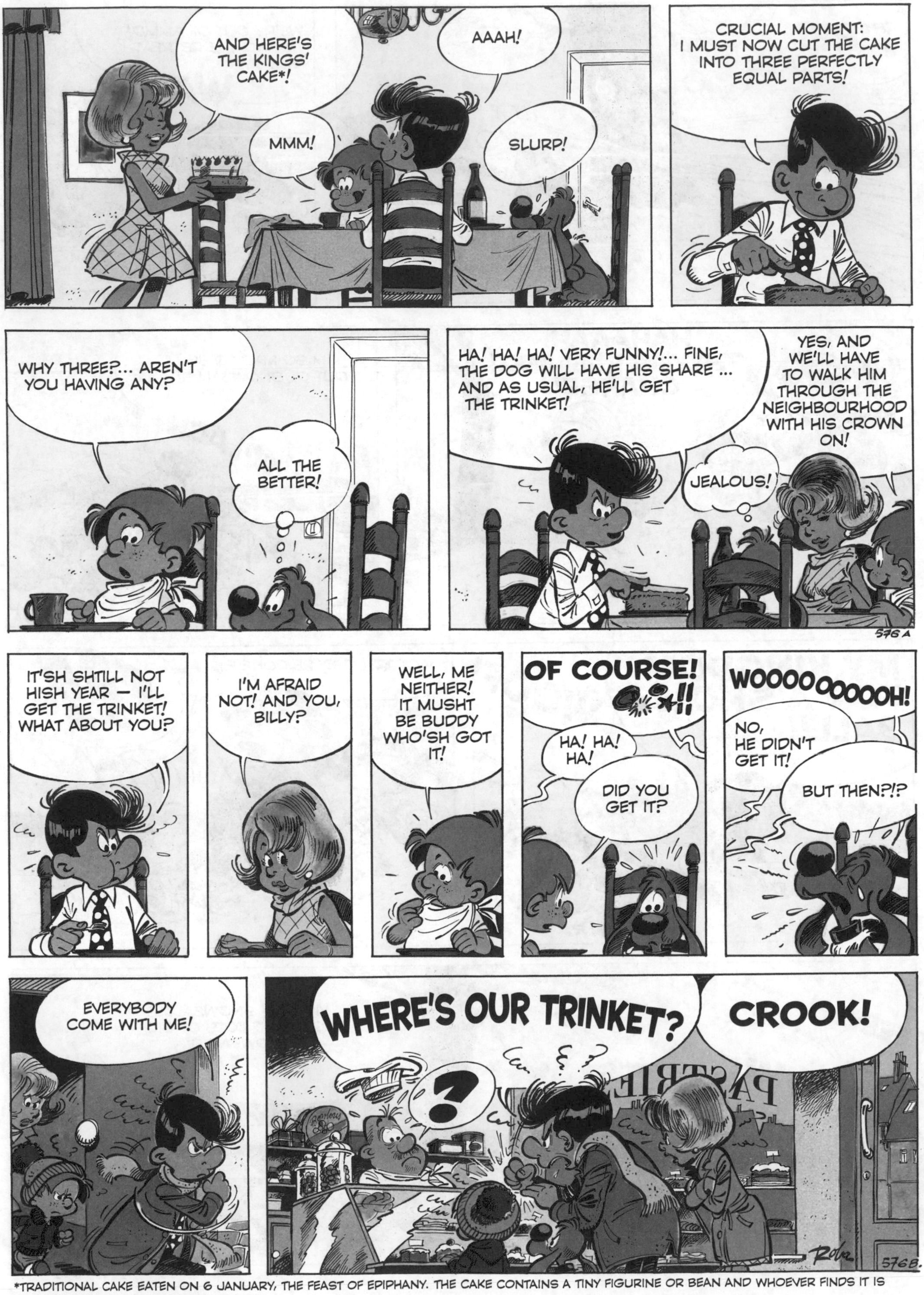
AND HERE'S THE KINGS' CAKE*!
MMM!
AAAH!
SLURP!
CRUCIAL MOMENT: I MUST NOW CUT THE CAKE INTO THREE PERFECTLY EQUAL PARTS!
WHY THREE?... AREN'T YOU HAVING ANY?
ALL THE BETTER!
HA! HA! HA! VERY FUNNY!... FINE, THE DOG WILL HAVE HIS SHARE ... AND AS USUAL, HE'LL GET THE TRINKET!
JEALOUS!
YES, AND WE'LL HAVE TO WALK HIM THROUGH THE NEIGHBOURHOOD WITH HIS CROWN ON!
576 A
IT'SH SHTILL NOT HISH YEAR — I'LL GET THE TRINKET! WHAT ABOUT YOU?
I'M AFRAID NOT! AND YOU, BILLY?
WELL, ME NEITHER! IT MUSHT BE BUDDY WHO'SH GOT IT!
OF COURSE!
HA! HA! HA!
DID YOU GET IT?
WOOOOOOOOOH!
NO, HE DIDN'T GET IT!
BUT THEN?!?
EVERYBODY COME WITH ME!
WHERE'S OUR TRINKET?
CROOK!
?
PASTRIES
Roba
576 B.

*TRADITIONAL CAKE EATEN ON 6 JANUARY, THE FEAST OF EPIPHANY. THE CAKE CONTAINS A TINY FIGURINE OR BEAN AND WHOEVER FINDS IT IS CROWNED KING OR QUEEN FOR THE DAY.

Secret weapon

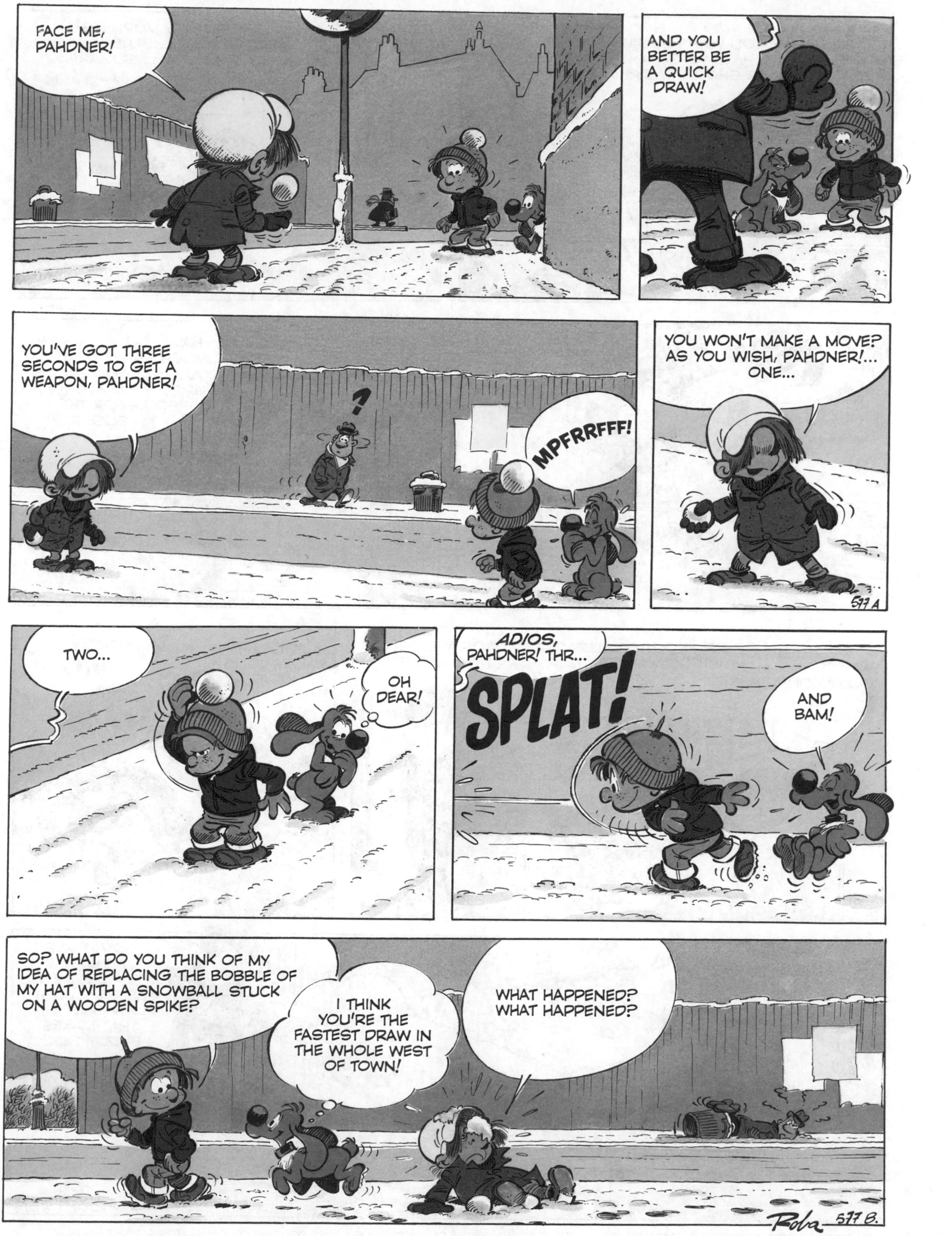
FACE ME, PAHDNER!
AND YOU BETTER BE A QUICK DRAW!
YOU'VE GOT THREE SECONDS TO GET A WEAPON, PAHDNER!
?
MPFRRFFF!
YOU WON'T MAKE A MOVE? AS YOU WISH, PAHDNER!... ONE...
577 A
TWO...
OH DEAR!
ADIOS, PAHDNER! THR...
SPLAT!
AND BAM!
SO? WHAT DO YOU THINK OF MY IDEA OF REPLACING THE BOBBLE OF MY HAT WITH A SNOWBALL STUCK ON A WOODEN SPIKE?
I THINK YOU'RE THE FASTEST DRAW IN THE WHOLE WEST OF TOWN!
WHAT HAPPENED? WHAT HAPPENED?
Roba 577 B.

Snowplough

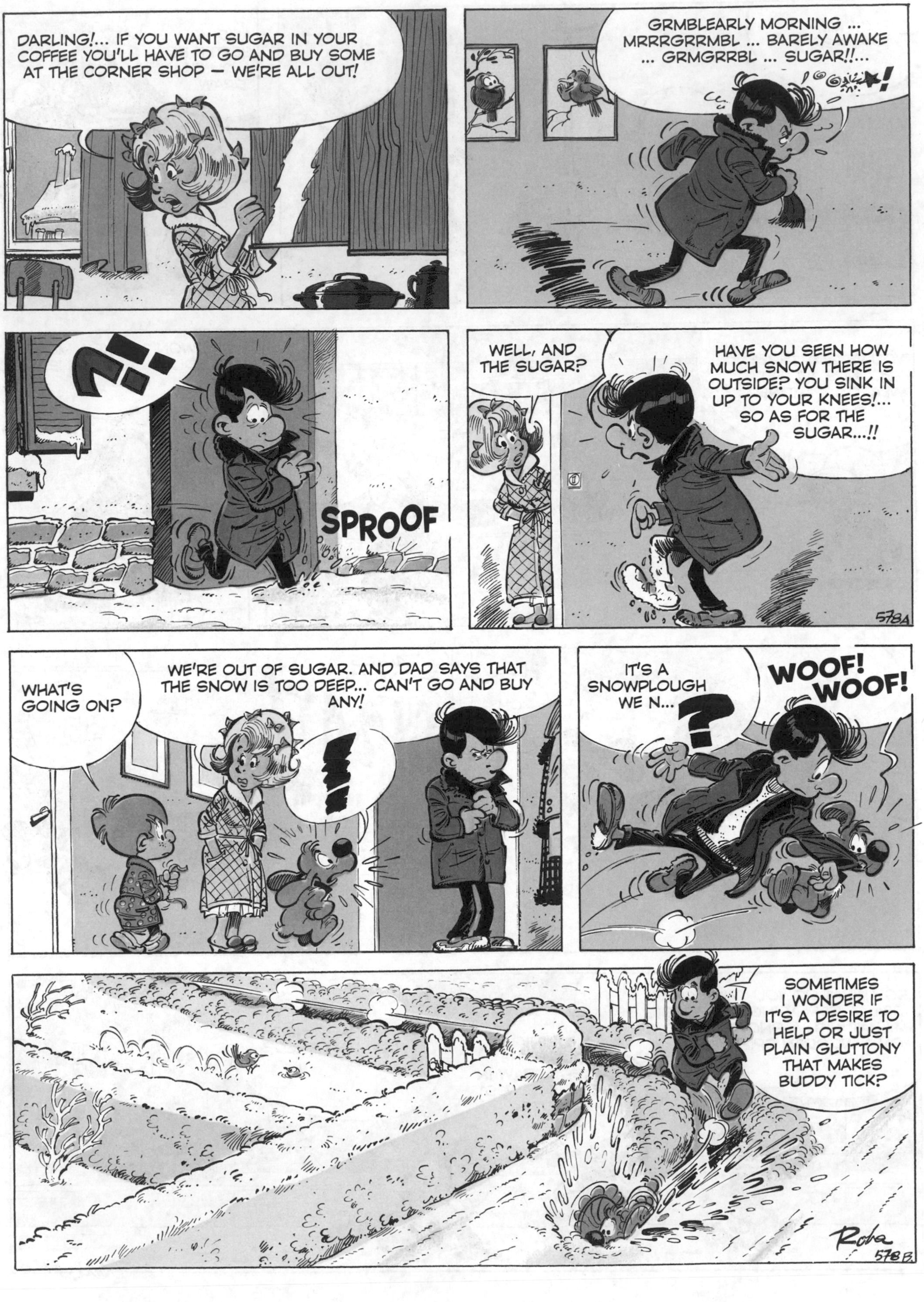
DARLING!... IF YOU WANT SUGAR IN YOUR COFFEE YOU'LL HAVE TO GO AND BUY SOME AT THE CORNER SHOP — WE'RE ALL OUT!
GRMBLEARLY MORNING ... MRRRGRRMBL ... BARELY AWAKE ... GRMGRRBL ... SUGAR!!...
SPROOF
WELL, AND THE SUGAR?
HAVE YOU SEEN HOW MUCH SNOW THERE IS OUTSIDE? YOU SINK IN UP TO YOUR KNEES!... SO AS FOR THE SUGAR...!!
578A
WHAT'S GOING ON?
WE'RE OUT OF SUGAR. AND DAD SAYS THAT THE SNOW IS TOO DEEP... CAN'T GO AND BUY ANY!
IT'S A SNOWPLOUGH WE N...
WOOF! WOOF!
SOMETIMES I WONDER IF IT'S A DESIRE TO HELP OR JUST PLAIN GLUTTONY THAT MAKES BUDDY TICK?
Roba
578 B.

Fresh air

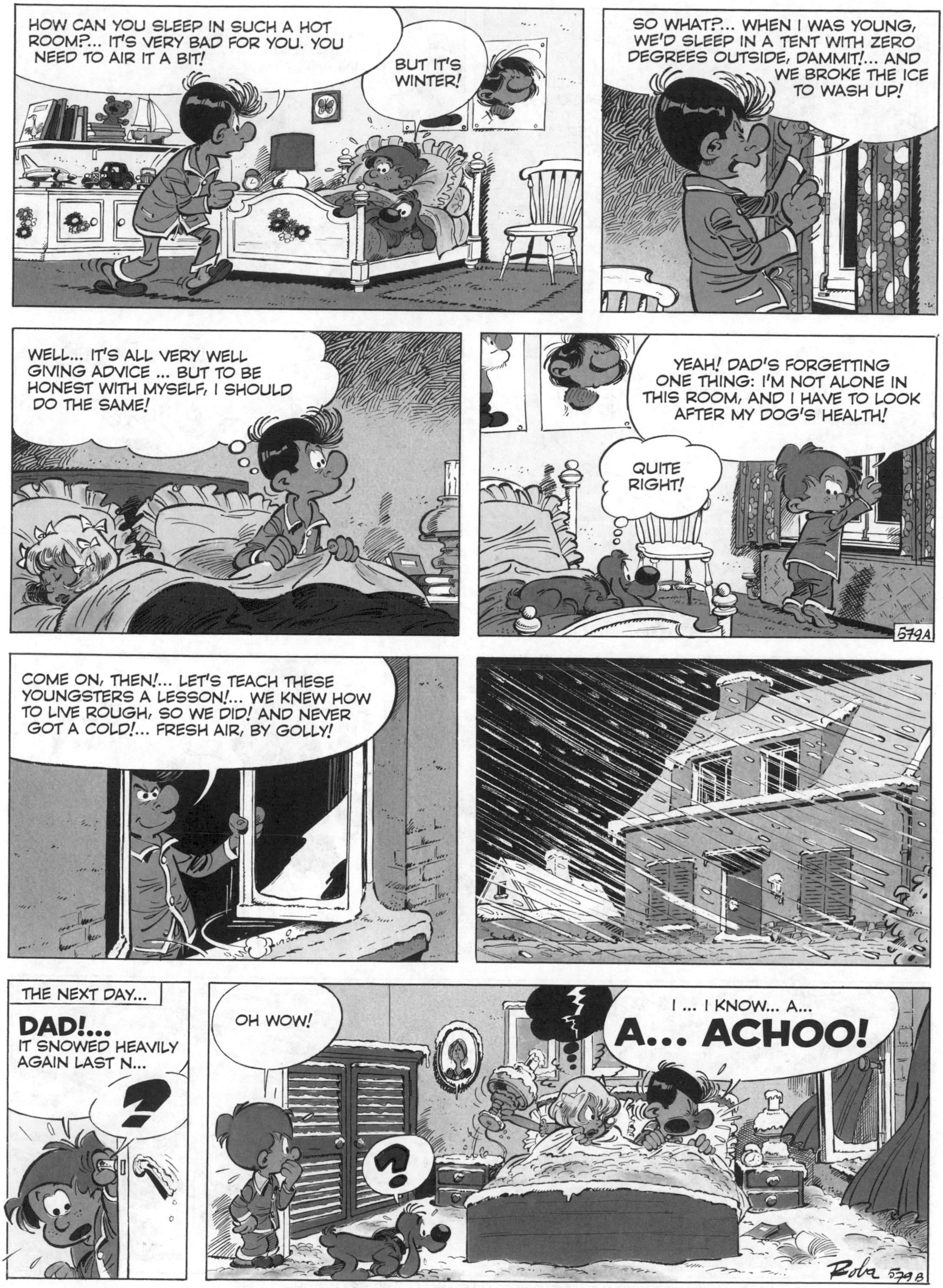

HOW CAN YOU SLEEP IN SUCH A HOT ROOM?... IT'S VERY BAD FOR YOU. YOU NEED TO AIR IT A BIT!
BUT IT'S WINTER!
SO WHAT?... WHEN I WAS YOUNG, WE'D SLEEP IN A TENT WITH ZERO DEGREES OUTSIDE, DAMMIT!... AND WE BROKE THE ICE TO WASH UP!
WELL... IT'S ALL VERY WELL GIVING ADVICE ... BUT TO BE HONEST WITH MYSELF, I SHOULD DO THE SAME!
YEAH! DAD'S FORGETTING ONE THING: I'M NOT ALONE IN THIS ROOM, AND I HAVE TO LOOK AFTER MY DOG'S HEALTH!
QUITE RIGHT!
579A
COME ON, THEN!... LET'S TEACH THESE YOUNGSTERS A LESSON!... WE KNEW HOW TO LIVE ROUGH, SO WE DID! AND NEVER GOT A COLD!... FRESH AIR, BY GOLLY!
THE NEXT DAY...
DAD!... IT SNOWED HEAVILY AGAIN LAST N...
?
OH WOW!
I ... I KNOW... A...
A... ACHOO!
?
Roba 579B

Seagulls

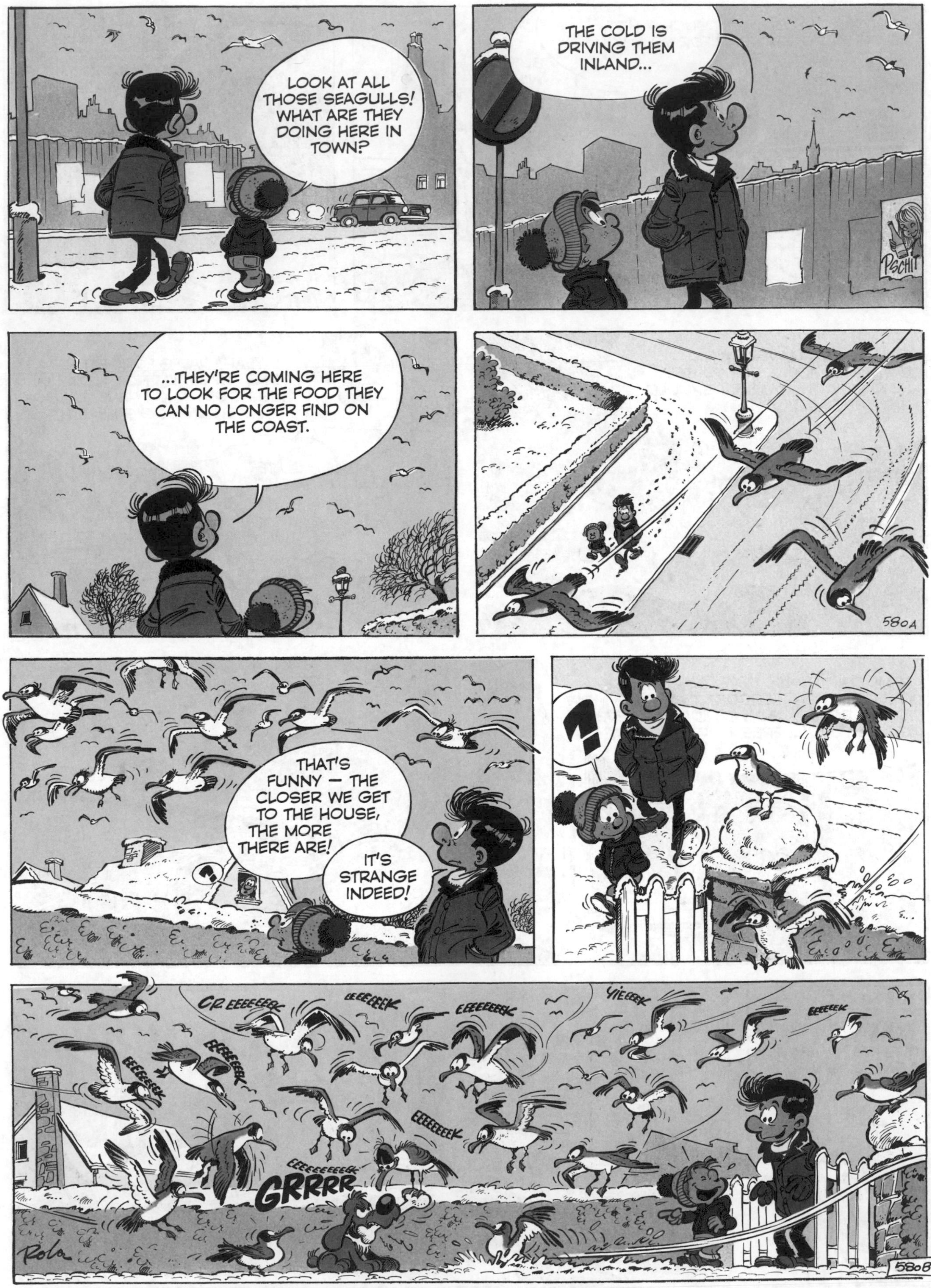
LOOK AT ALL THOSE SEAGULLS! WHAT ARE THEY DOING HERE IN TOWN?
THE COLD IS DRIVING THEM INLAND...
PSCHIT
...THEY'RE COMING HERE TO LOOK FOR THE FOOD THEY CAN NO LONGER FIND ON THE COAST.
580A
THAT'S FUNNY — THE CLOSER WE GET TO THE HOUSE, THE MORE THERE ARE!
IT'S STRANGE INDEED!
?
YIEEEK
GRRRR
Rola
580B

STARRING THE 'LAUGHING GULL', WITH THE KIND AUTHORISATION OF MR FRANQUIN AND MR GASTON.

Stiff neck

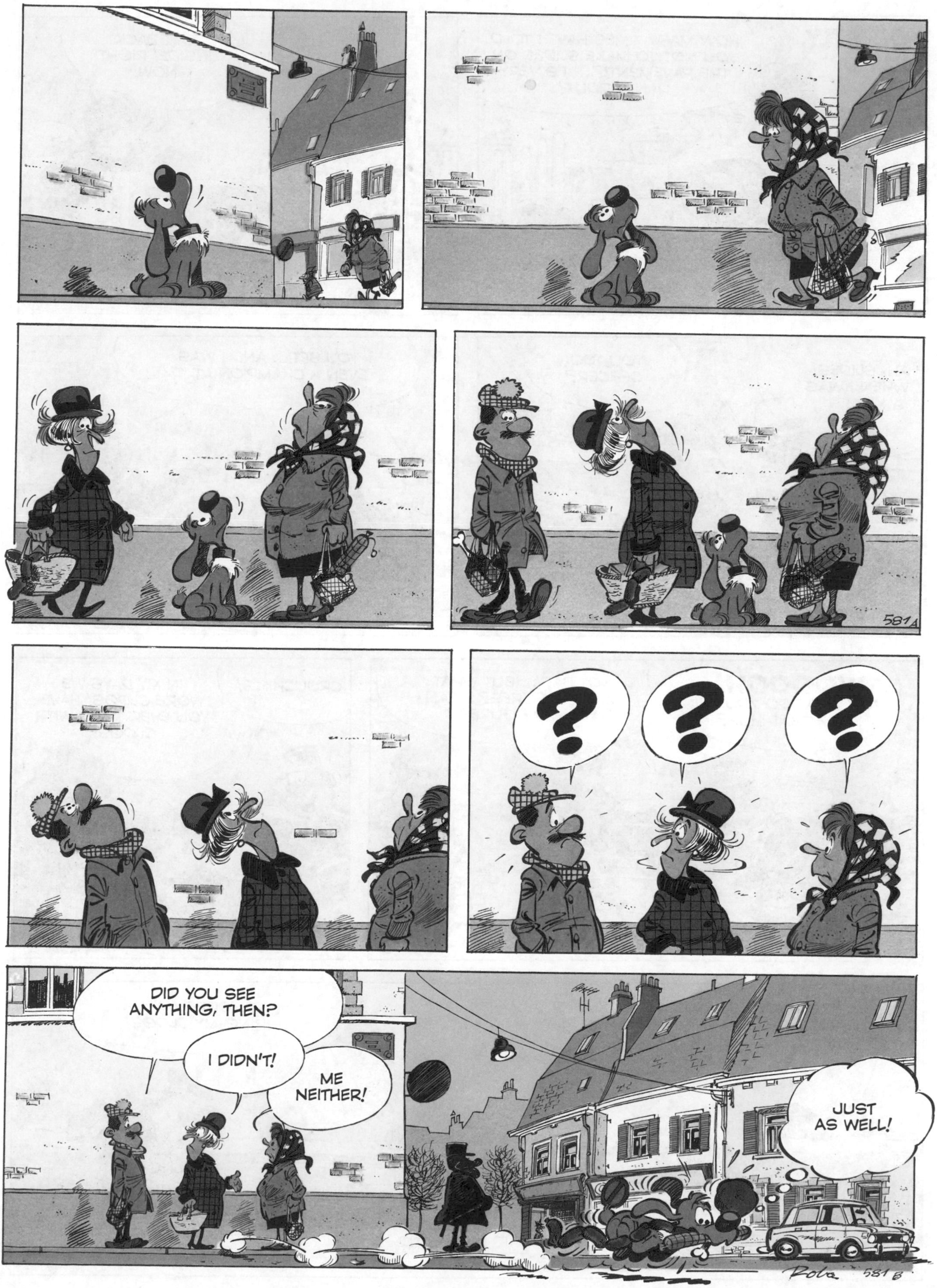
?
?
?
DID YOU SEE ANYTHING, THEN?
I DIDN'T!
ME NEITHER!
JUST AS WELL!

Let's slide...

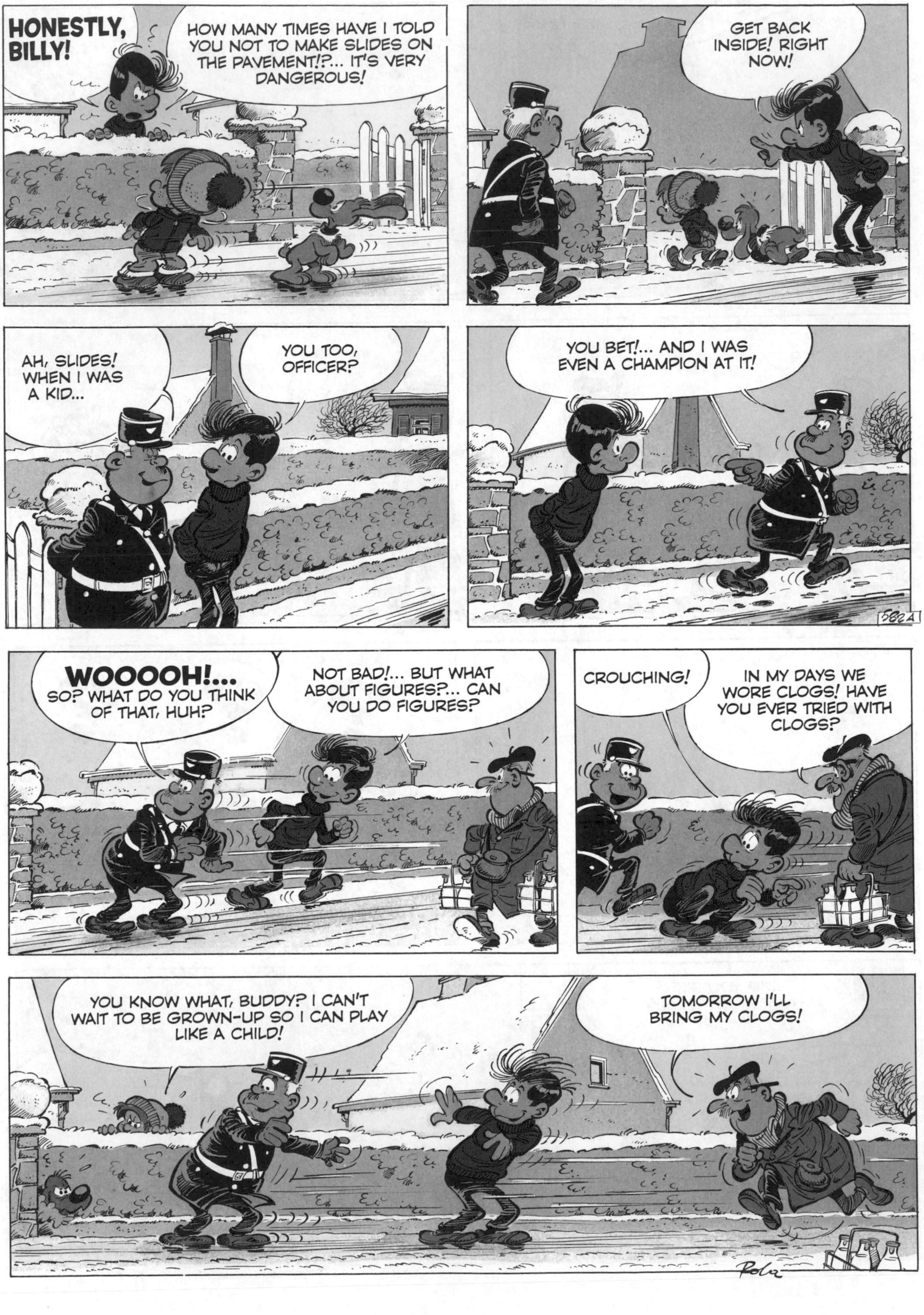

HONESTLY, BILLY!
HOW MANY TIMES HAVE I TOLD YOU NOT TO MAKE SLIDES ON THE PAVEMENT!?... IT'S VERY DANGEROUS!
GET BACK INSIDE! RIGHT NOW!
AH, SLIDES! WHEN I WAS A KID...
YOU TOO, OFFICER?
YOU BET!... AND I WAS EVEN A CHAMPION AT IT!
WOOOOH!... SO? WHAT DO YOU THINK OF THAT, HUH?
NOT BAD!... BUT WHAT ABOUT FIGURES?... CAN YOU DO FIGURES?
CROUCHING!
IN MY DAYS WE WORE CLOGS! HAVE YOU EVER TRIED WITH CLOGS?
YOU KNOW WHAT, BUDDY? I CAN'T WAIT TO BE GROWN-UP SO I CAN PLAY LIKE A CHILD!
TOMORROW I'LL BRING MY CLOGS!

Bon appétit

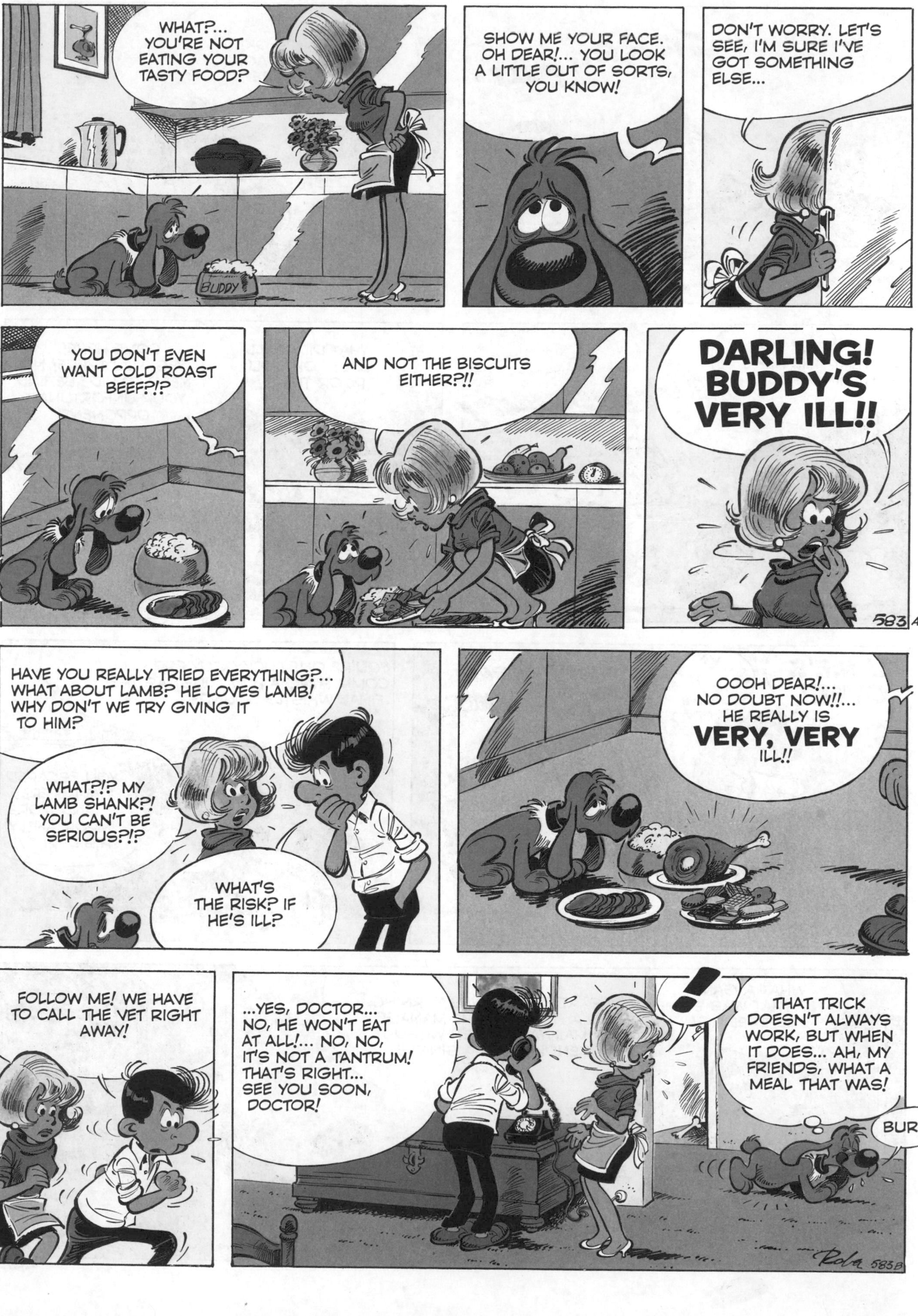

WHAT?... YOU'RE NOT EATING YOUR TASTY FOOD?
BUDDY
SHOW ME YOUR FACE. OH DEAR!... YOU LOOK A LITTLE OUT OF SORTS, YOU KNOW!
DON'T WORRY. LET'S SEE, I'M SURE I'VE GOT SOMETHING ELSE...
YOU DON'T EVEN WANT COLD ROAST BEEF?!?
AND NOT THE BISCUITS EITHER?!!
DARLING! BUDDY'S VERY ILL!!
583 A
HAVE YOU REALLY TRIED EVERYTHING?... WHAT ABOUT LAMB? HE LOVES LAMB! WHY DON'T WE TRY GIVING IT TO HIM?
WHAT?!? MY LAMB SHANK?! YOU CAN'T BE SERIOUS?!?
WHAT'S THE RISK? IF HE'S ILL?
OOOH DEAR!... NO DOUBT NOW!!... HE REALLY IS VERY, VERY ILL!!
FOLLOW ME! WE HAVE TO CALL THE VET RIGHT AWAY!
...YES, DOCTOR... NO, HE WON'T EAT AT ALL!... NO, NO, IT'S NOT A TANTRUM! THAT'S RIGHT... SEE YOU SOON, DOCTOR!
!
THAT TRICK DOESN'T ALWAYS WORK, BUT WHEN IT DOES... AH, MY FRIENDS, WHAT A MEAL THAT WAS!
BURP!
Roba
583 B

Whistle of doom

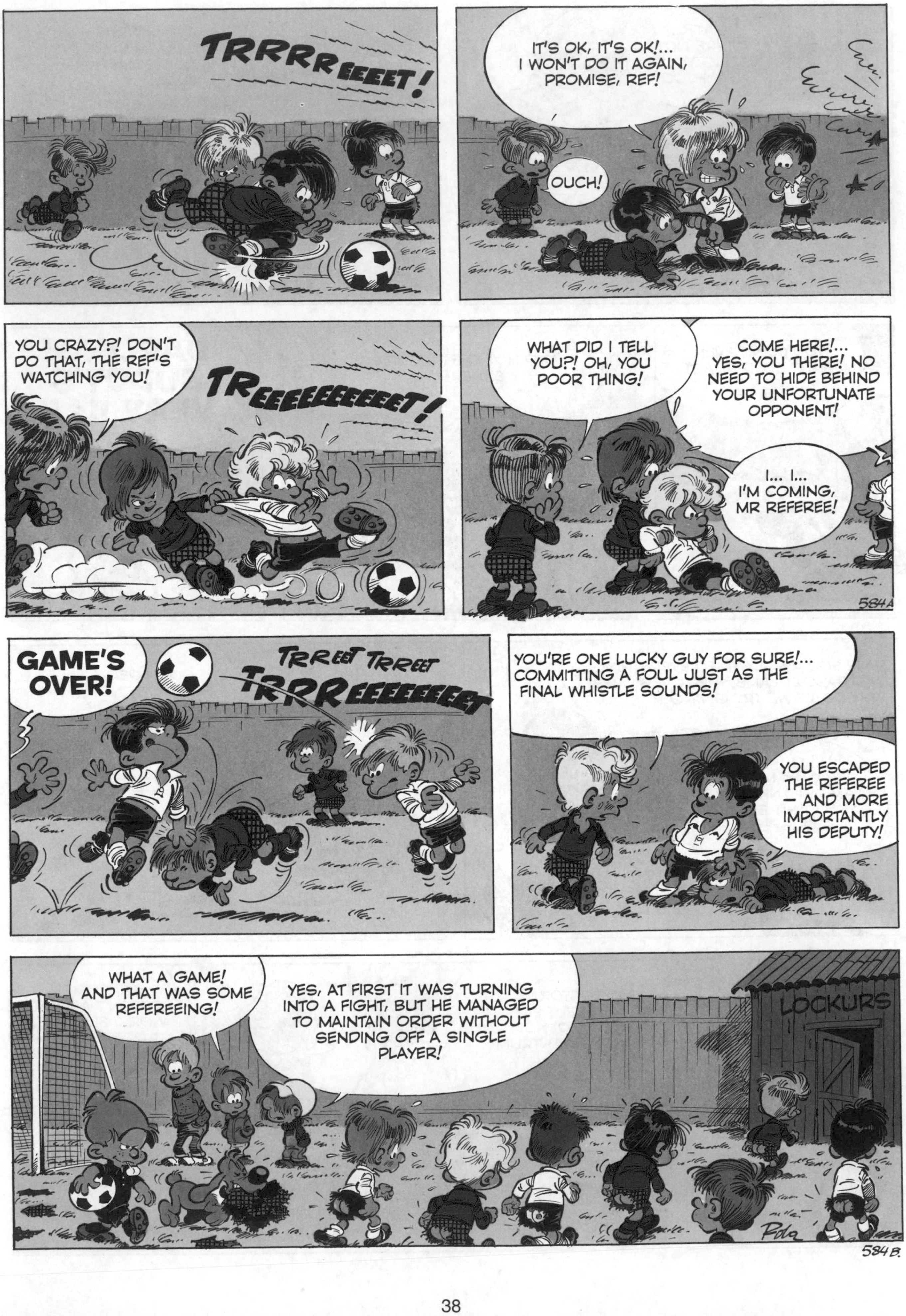
TRRRREEEET!
IT'S OK, IT'S OK!... I WON'T DO IT AGAIN, PROMISE, REF!
OUCH!
YOU CRAZY?! DON'T DO THAT, THE REF'S WATCHING YOU!
TREEEEEEEEEET!
WHAT DID I TELL YOU?! OH, YOU POOR THING!
COME HERE!... YES, YOU THERE! NO NEED TO HIDE BEHIND YOUR UNFORTUNATE OPPONENT!
I... I... I'M COMING, MR REFEREE!
584A
GAME'S OVER!
TRREET TRREET TRRREEEEEEEET
YOU'RE ONE LUCKY GUY FOR SURE!... COMMITTING A FOUL JUST AS THE FINAL WHISTLE SOUNDS!
YOU ESCAPED THE REFEREE — AND MORE IMPORTANTLY HIS DEPUTY!
WHAT A GAME! AND THAT WAS SOME REFEREEING!
YES, AT FIRST IT WAS TURNING INTO A FIGHT, BUT HE MANAGED TO MAINTAIN ORDER WITHOUT SENDING OFF A SINGLE PLAYER!
LOCKURS
584B.

The great illusion

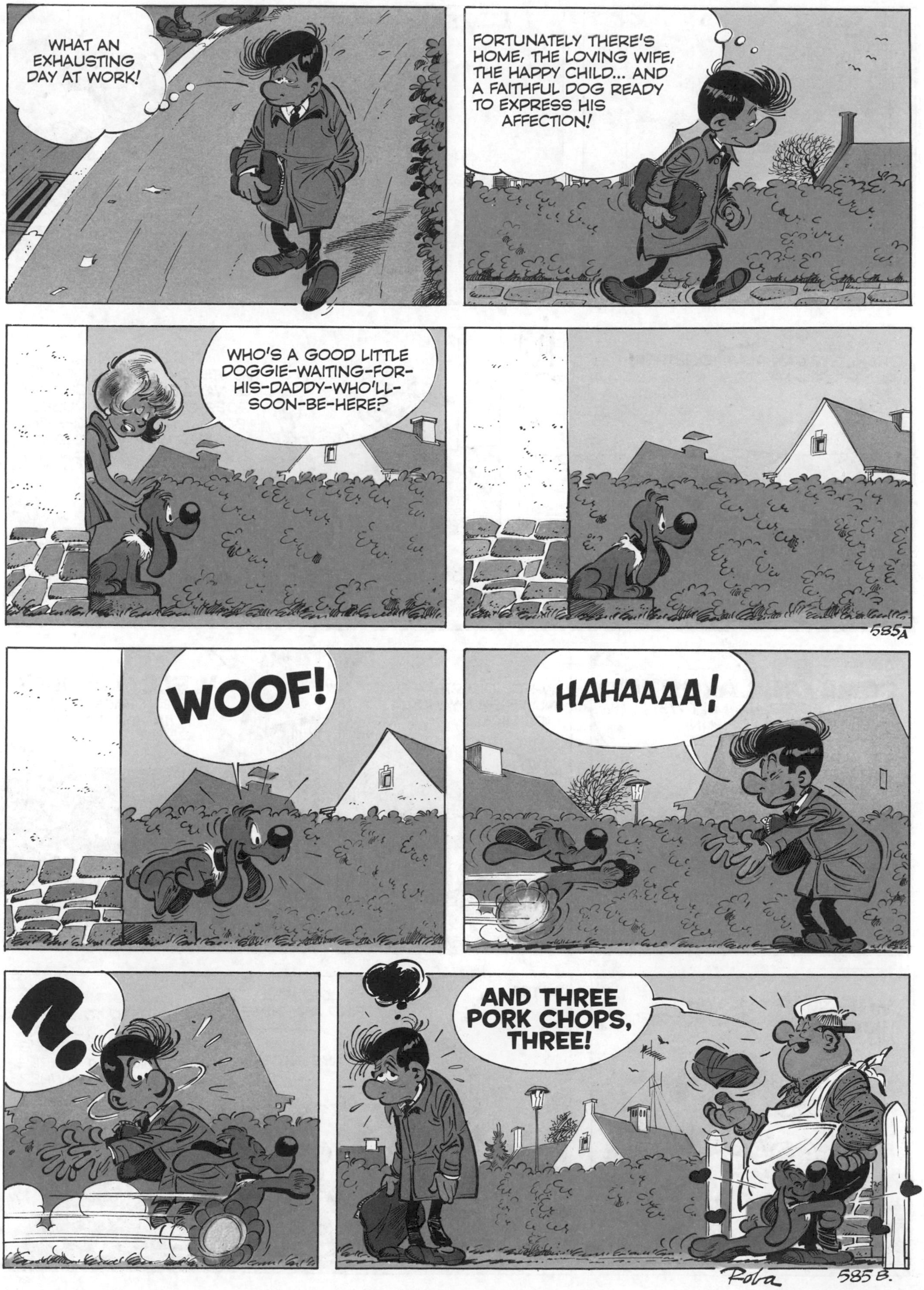
WHAT AN EXHAUSTING DAY AT WORK!
FORTUNATELY THERE'S HOME, THE LOVING WIFE, THE HAPPY CHILD... AND A FAITHFUL DOG READY TO EXPRESS HIS AFFECTION!
WHO'S A GOOD LITTLE DOGGIE-WAITING-FOR-HIS-DADDY-WHO'LL-SOON-BE-HERE?
585A
WOOF!
HAHAAAA!
?
AND THREE PORK CHOPS, THREE!
Roba
585 B.

Sleepcrawling

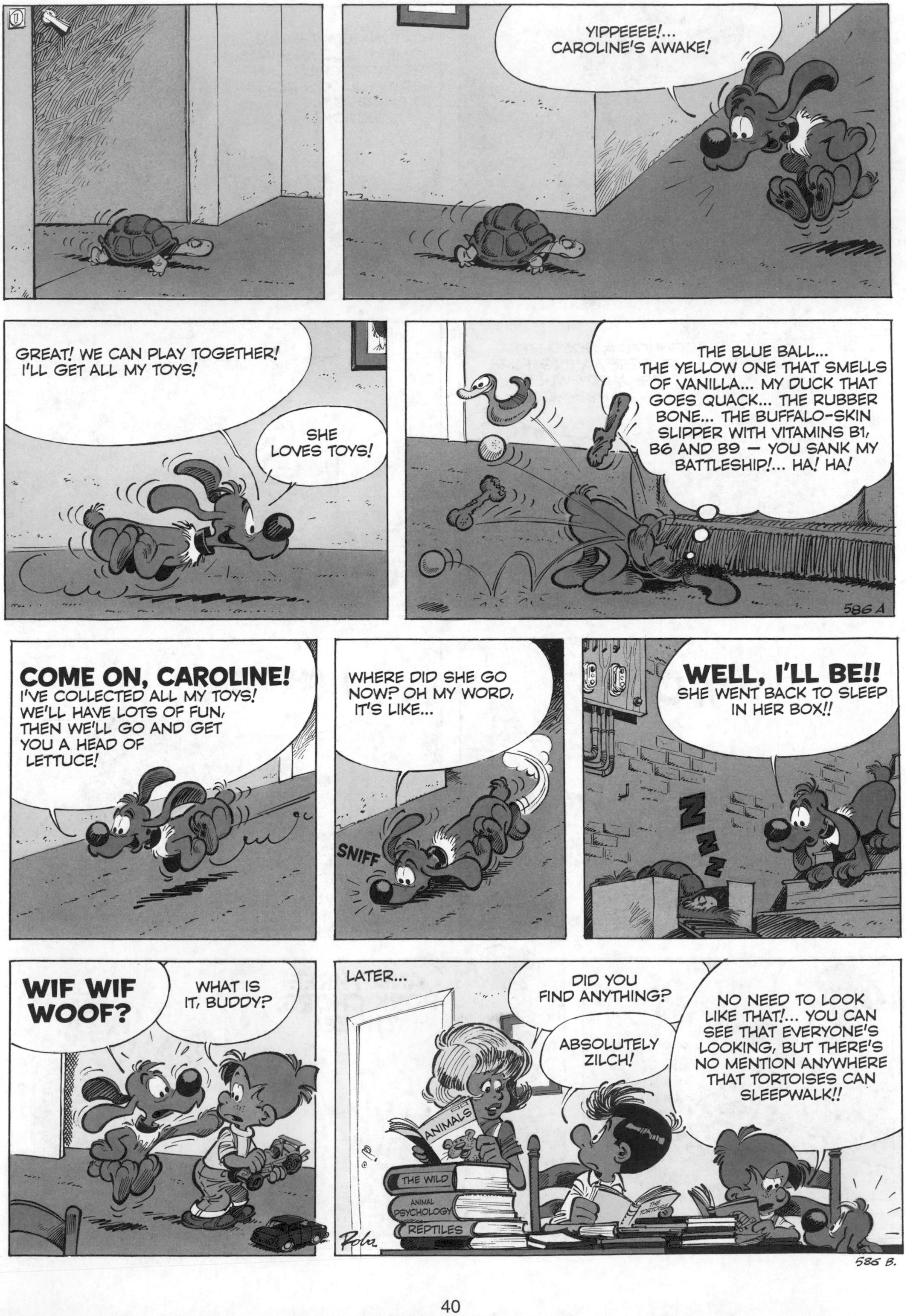
YIPPEEEE!... CAROLINE'S AWAKE!
GREAT! WE CAN PLAY TOGETHER! I'LL GET ALL MY TOYS!
SHE LOVES TOYS!
THE BLUE BALL... THE YELLOW ONE THAT SMELLS OF VANILLA... MY DUCK THAT GOES QUACK... THE RUBBER BONE... THE BUFFALO-SKIN SLIPPER WITH VITAMINS B1, B6 AND B9 — YOU SANK MY BATTLESHIP!... HA! HA!
586 A
COME ON, CAROLINE! I'VE COLLECTED ALL MY TOYS! WE'LL HAVE LOTS OF FUN, THEN WE'LL GO AND GET YOU A HEAD OF LETTUCE!
WHERE DID SHE GO NOW? OH MY WORD, IT'S LIKE...
SNIFF
WELL, I'LL BE!! SHE WENT BACK TO SLEEP IN HER BOX!!
Z Z Z
WIF WIF WOOF?
WHAT IS IT, BUDDY?
LATER...
DID YOU FIND ANYTHING?
ABSOLUTELY ZILCH!
NO NEED TO LOOK LIKE THAT!... YOU CAN SEE THAT EVERYONE'S LOOKING, BUT THERE'S NO MENTION ANYWHERE THAT TORTOISES CAN SLEEPWALK!!
ANIMALS
THE WILD
ANIMAL PSYCHOLOGY
REPTILES
THE TORTOISE
Roba
586 B.

Spring

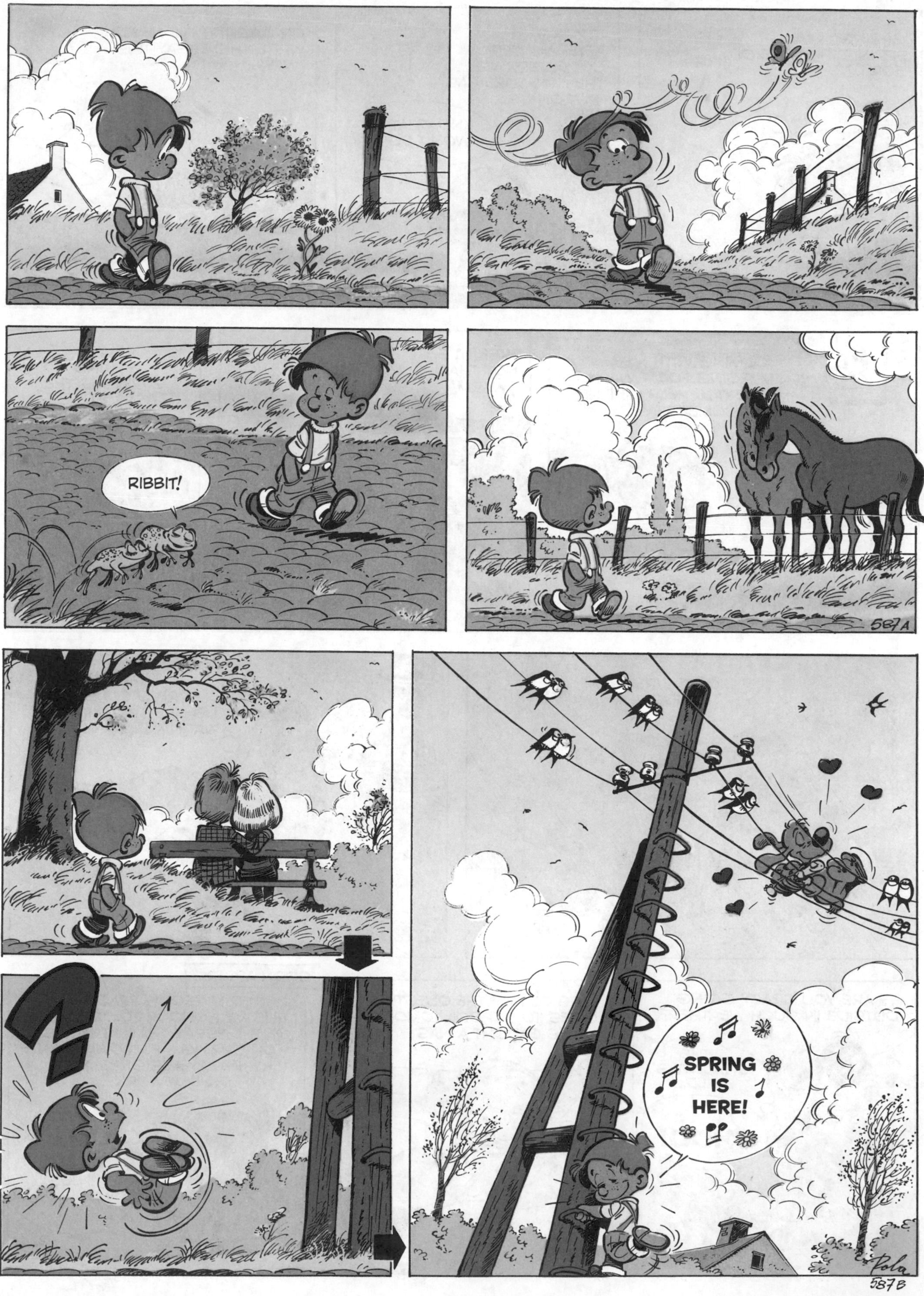
RIBBIT!
SPRING IS HERE!

Inspiration

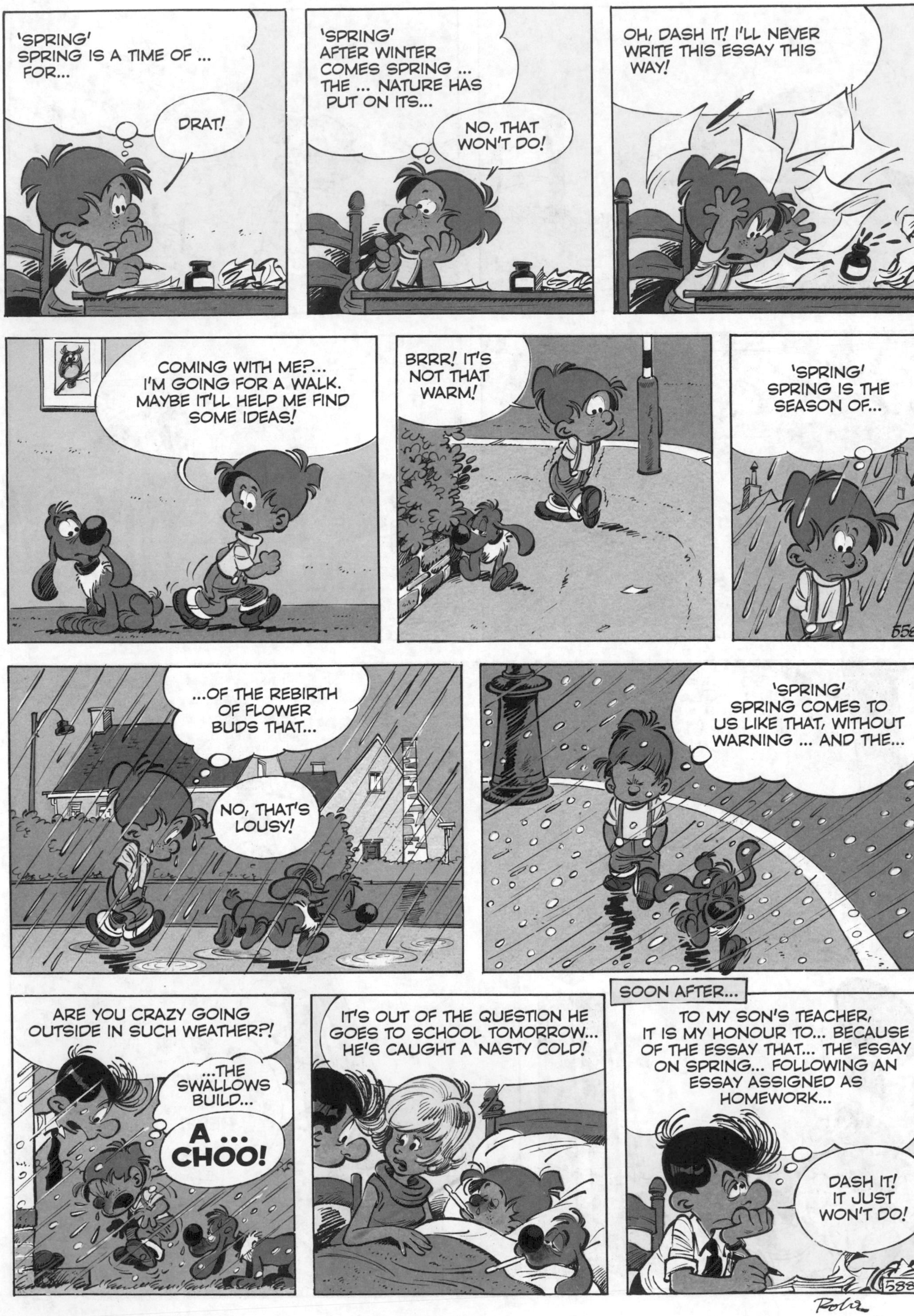

'SPRING'
SPRING IS A TIME OF ... FOR...
DRAT!
'SPRING'
AFTER WINTER COMES SPRING ... THE ... NATURE HAS PUT ON ITS...
NO, THAT WON'T DO!
OH, DASH IT! I'LL NEVER WRITE THIS ESSAY THIS WAY!
COMING WITH ME?... I'M GOING FOR A WALK. MAYBE IT'LL HELP ME FIND SOME IDEAS!
BRRR! IT'S NOT THAT WARM!
'SPRING'
SPRING IS THE SEASON OF...
...OF THE REBIRTH OF FLOWER BUDS THAT...
NO, THAT'S LOUSY!
'SPRING'
SPRING COMES TO US LIKE THAT, WITHOUT WARNING ... AND THE...
ARE YOU CRAZY GOING OUTSIDE IN SUCH WEATHER?!
...THE SWALLOWS BUILD...
A ... CHOO!
IT'S OUT OF THE QUESTION HE GOES TO SCHOOL TOMORROW... HE'S CAUGHT A NASTY COLD!
SOON AFTER...
TO MY SON'S TEACHER, IT IS MY HONOUR TO... BECAUSE OF THE ESSAY THAT... THE ESSAY ON SPRING... FOLLOWING AN ESSAY ASSIGNED AS HOMEWORK...
DASH IT! IT JUST WON'T DO!

Airbrushing

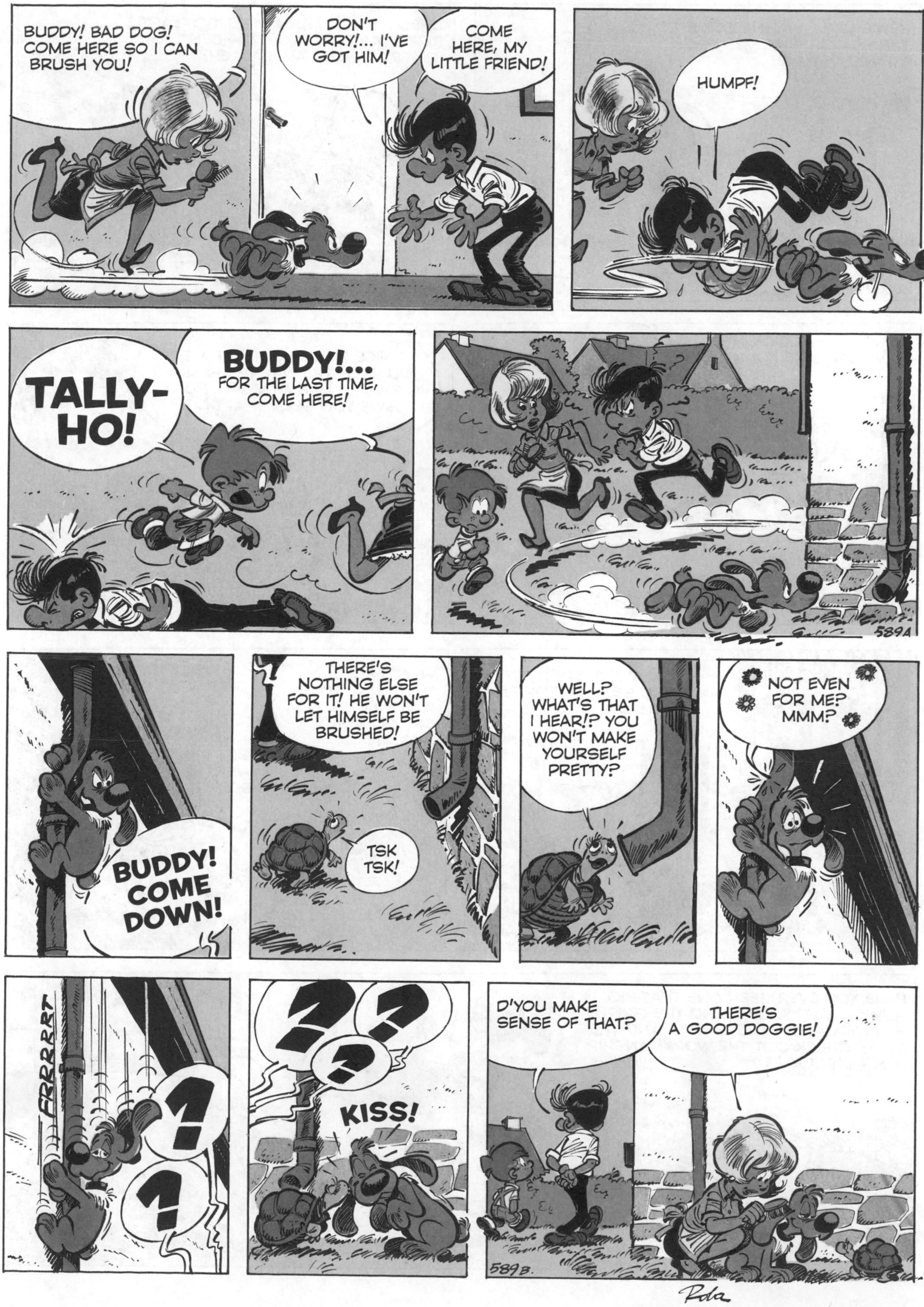

BUDDY! BAD DOG! COME HERE SO I CAN BRUSH YOU!
DON'T WORRY!... I'VE GOT HIM!
COME HERE, MY LITTLE FRIEND!
HUMPF!
TALLY-HO!
BUDDY!... FOR THE LAST TIME, COME HERE!
589A
BUDDY! COME DOWN!
THERE'S NOTHING ELSE FOR IT! HE WON'T LET HIMSELF BE BRUSHED!
TSK TSK!
WELL? WHAT'S THAT I HEAR!? YOU WON'T MAKE YOURSELF PRETTY?
NOT EVEN FOR ME? MMM?
FRRRRRT
KISS!
D'YOU MAKE SENSE OF THAT?
THERE'S A GOOD DOGGIE!
589B.
Roba

What a pistol!

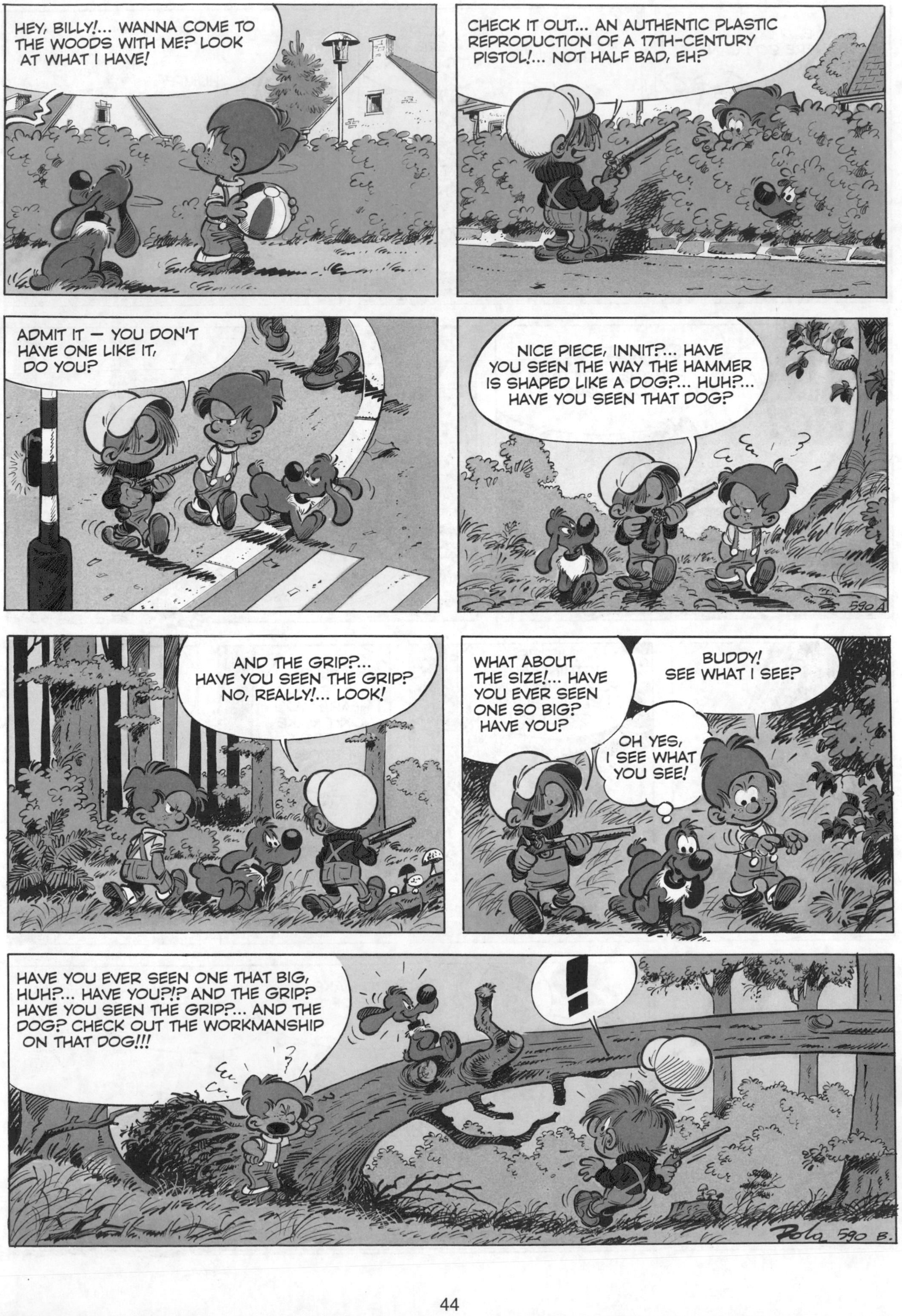

HEY, BILLY!... WANNA COME TO THE WOODS WITH ME? LOOK AT WHAT I HAVE!
CHECK IT OUT... AN AUTHENTIC PLASTIC REPRODUCTION OF A 17TH-CENTURY PISTOL!... NOT HALF BAD, EH?
ADMIT IT — YOU DON'T HAVE ONE LIKE IT, DO YOU?
NICE PIECE, INNIT?... HAVE YOU SEEN THE WAY THE HAMMER IS SHAPED LIKE A DOG?... HUH?... HAVE YOU SEEN THAT DOG?
AND THE GRIP?... HAVE YOU SEEN THE GRIP? NO, REALLY!... LOOK!
WHAT ABOUT THE SIZE!... HAVE YOU EVER SEEN ONE SO BIG? HAVE YOU?
BUDDY! SEE WHAT I SEE?
OH YES, I SEE WHAT YOU SEE!
HAVE YOU EVER SEEN ONE THAT BIG, HUH?... HAVE YOU?!? AND THE GRIP? HAVE YOU SEEN THE GRIP?... AND THE DOG? CHECK OUT THE WORKMANSHIP ON THAT DOG!!!
!

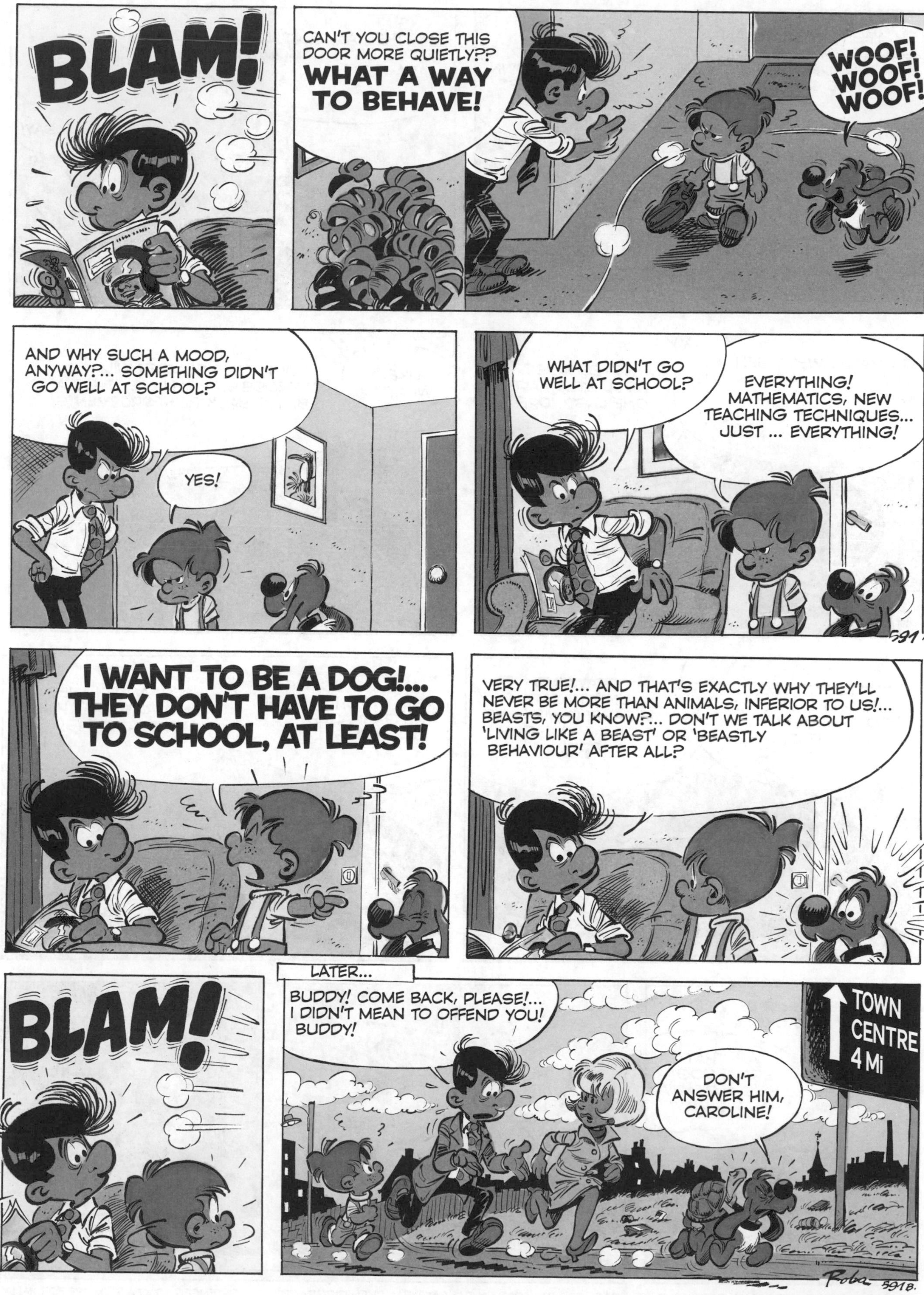
BLAM!
CAN'T YOU CLOSE THIS DOOR MORE QUIETLY?? WHAT A WAY TO BEHAVE!
WOOF! WOOF! WOOF!
AND WHY SUCH A MOOD, ANYWAY?... SOMETHING DIDN'T GO WELL AT SCHOOL?
YES!
WHAT DIDN'T GO WELL AT SCHOOL?
EVERYTHING! MATHEMATICS, NEW TEACHING TECHNIQUES... JUST ... EVERYTHING!
I WANT TO BE A DOG!... THEY DON'T HAVE TO GO TO SCHOOL, AT LEAST!
VERY TRUE!... AND THAT'S EXACTLY WHY THEY'LL NEVER BE MORE THAN ANIMALS, INFERIOR TO US!... BEASTS, YOU KNOW?... DON'T WE TALK ABOUT 'LIVING LIKE A BEAST' OR 'BEASTLY BEHAVIOUR' AFTER ALL?
BLAM!
LATER...
BUDDY! COME BACK, PLEASE!... I DIDN'T MEAN TO OFFEND YOU! BUDDY!
TOWN CENTRE 4 Mi
DON'T ANSWER HIM, CAROLINE!
Roba

Courage under fire

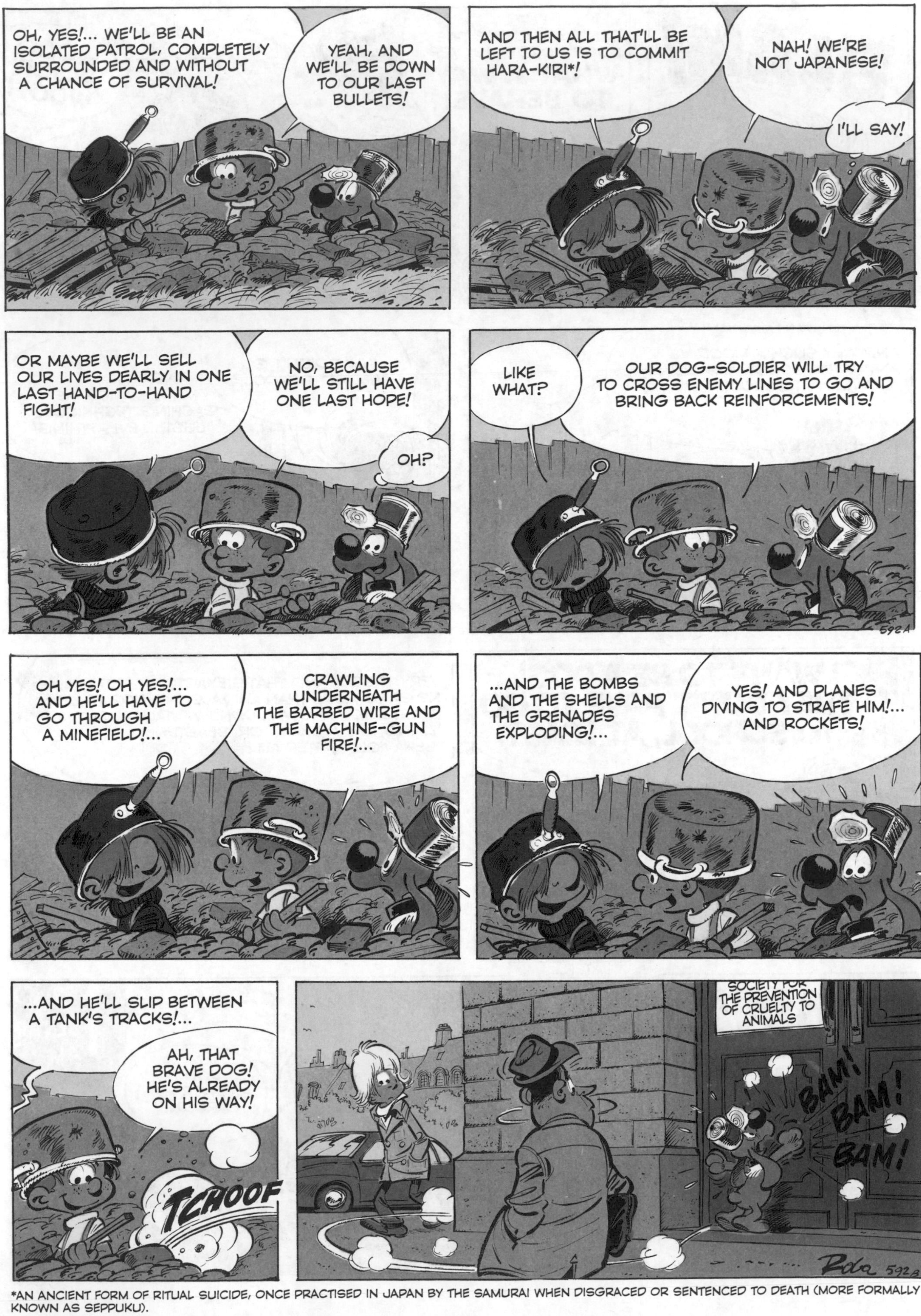
OH, YES!... WE'LL BE AN ISOLATED PATROL, COMPLETELY SURROUNDED AND WITHOUT A CHANCE OF SURVIVAL!
YEAH, AND WE'LL BE DOWN TO OUR LAST BULLETS!
AND THEN ALL THAT'LL BE LEFT TO US IS TO COMMIT HARA-KIRI*!
NAH! WE'RE NOT JAPANESE!
I'LL SAY!
OR MAYBE WE'LL SELL OUR LIVES DEARLY IN ONE LAST HAND-TO-HAND FIGHT!
NO, BECAUSE WE'LL STILL HAVE ONE LAST HOPE!
OH?
LIKE WHAT?
OUR DOG-SOLDIER WILL TRY TO CROSS ENEMY LINES TO GO AND BRING BACK REINFORCEMENTS!
592 A
OH YES! OH YES!... AND HE'LL HAVE TO GO THROUGH A MINEFIELD!...
CRAWLING UNDERNEATH THE BARBED WIRE AND THE MACHINE-GUN FIRE!...
...AND THE BOMBS AND THE SHELLS AND THE GRENADES EXPLODING!...
YES! AND PLANES DIVING TO STRAFE HIM!... AND ROCKETS!
...AND HE'LL SLIP BETWEEN A TANK'S TRACKS!...
AH, THAT BRAVE DOG! HE'S ALREADY ON HIS WAY!
TCHOOF
SOCIETY FOR THE PREVENTION OF CRUELTY TO ANIMALS
BAM!
BAM!
BAM!
Roba 592 B

*AN ANCIENT FORM OF RITUAL SUICIDE, ONCE PRACTISED IN JAPAN BY THE SAMURAI WHEN DISGRACED OR SENTENCED TO DEATH (MORE FORMALLY KNOWN AS SEPPUKU).

Billy & Buddy

1 — Billy & Buddy — REMEMBER THIS, BUDDY?

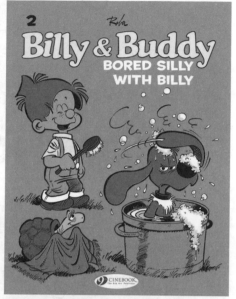

2 — Billy & Buddy — BORED SILLY WITH BILLY

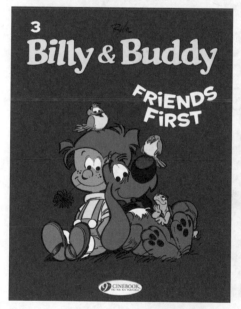

3 — Billy & Buddy — FRIENDS FIRST

4 — Billy & Buddy — IT'S A DOG'S LIFE

9th CINEBOOK
The 9th Art Publisher

www.cinebook.com

Billy & Buddy

COMING SOON

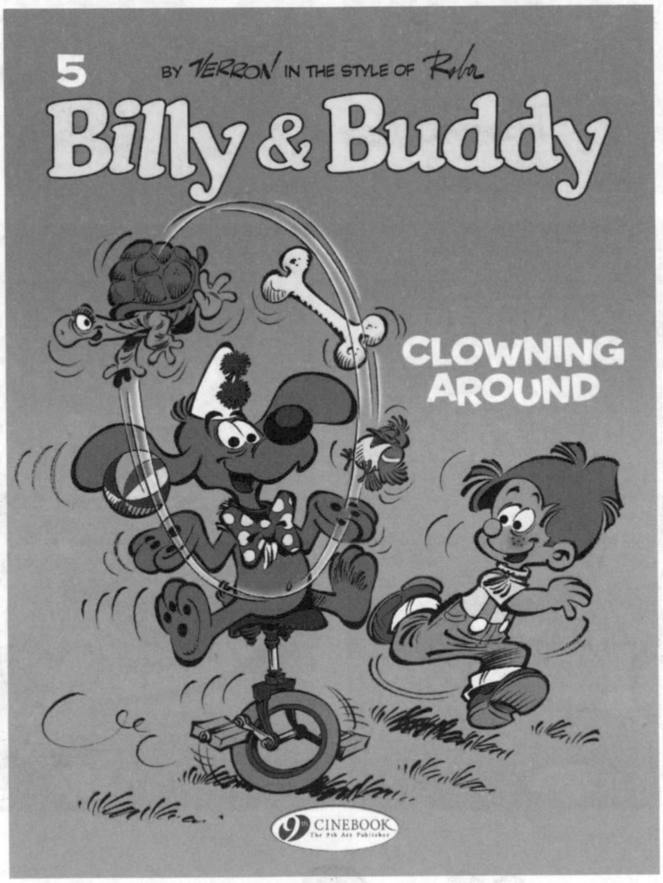
5
BY VERRON IN THE STYLE OF Roba
Billy & Buddy
CLOWNING AROUND
CINEBOOK
The 9th Art Publisher